THE STC MYSTERIES

-3-

MEAT IS MURDER

CHRIS MCDONALD

**RED DOG
UK**

Published by RED DOG PRESS 2021

First Edition

Hardback ISBN 978-1-914480-48-5
Paperback ISBN 978-1-914480-06-5
Ebook ISBN 978-1-914480-07-2

www.reddogpress.co.uk

1

CHICKEN

A FINE EXAMPLE of Northern Ireland's famous summers was in full bloom—there had been an hour of glorious sunshine in the morning, followed by a biblical downpour.

Despite the rain, Tyler Love smiled as the padlock clicked into place. He gave his comrade, who was now chained to the fence, a pat on the shoulder before walking up the line of bodies like he was their military commander.

He grinned at each person in turn as he passed by, and doled out words of passion.

We are The History Makers.

That caused a cheer that gave Tyler a boost. Not that he needed one—he already felt like John Wayne.

Change is not a threat, it's an opportunity.

No cheer this time.

Hmm. Probably a bit too wordy for these simpletons, he thought.

He raised a fist and some of his crew gave him a stoic nod in return, their minds turning to the task at hand, though really there wasn't too much to think about. All they had to do was make sure that the owners of the abattoir and the investor whose teat they planned on suckling from couldn't access the property.

When Tyler got to the end of the line, he bent down and stroked the cheek of the last protester. Helena lifted her chin and met Tyler's eyes, fire blazing in her own. He pressed his lips against hers and then refocused himself on what he was here to do.

He marched to the gate of the abattoir and pulled the chain around his middle. It was thicker than the others, more heavy-duty. It wasn't needed, particularly, but it was an effective subliminal way of showing that he was making the biggest statement.

If it wasn't for this great hunk of metal holding me back, there'd be no chance for these butchers of death.

That's the message he wanted to give off.

Making sure it wasn't too tight, he slipped the padlock in between two links and pressed down, securing himself in place.

He looked down the line at his fellow bunch of rag-tags, all giving up their Saturday for the greater good. The T-shirts had been a great idea, though he had been loath to admit it—giving Willow praise always seemed to upset the power balance in the group. He didn't want to give her any ideas that he was willing to relinquish the leader role.

Still, each member of the group had a lettered shirt that spelled out MEAT IS MURDER. It was a powerful message, and one he hoped would make a difference. It would look great on the cover of the local newspaper, for a start.

He looked out at the small crowd that had gathered, and tried not to be too disheartened. He thought that their social media blitz, alongside the adverts they'd placed in the Stonebridge Chronicle, might've encouraged more of the town's residents to join their protest.

But, there was still time before the real action began. Some of the undecided might make their way to this side of town just in time.

He glanced to his left again and noticed Helena staring at him with a strange look on her face. He smiled at her and she returned it, though there was something in her look that was gnawing at him.

Was she still thinking about their argument last week?

He turned away from her. There was nothing he could do about that now and, besides, there were bigger fish to fry today.

Not that frying fish would go down well with this group.

Wanting to do something, he called for one of the protesters who had opted to carry a placard, having wimped out of being chained up, and asked them to pass him the megaphone.

He grabbed it off her and turned it on. It emitted a shrill screech that caused some of the onlookers to jump in shock.

'People of Stonebridge, we, The History Makers, are here today to make a change. McNulty's Meats has been in the news over the past few years for all the wrong reasons. There have been allegations of animal cruelty, poor working conditions and unfair redundancies. And now, perhaps the worst of all, Kevin and Ron McNulty, the owners of this abomination,' he stopped and turned his head to the grey blocky building behind him, 'are planning to sell to a multinational.'

He stopped to allow his words to sink in. The rumours had been swirling around the town for weeks that the McNulty brothers were planning on selling up. A huge business from England with a worldwide reach had apparently approached the two brothers with an offer they couldn't refuse.

When the murmurings had abated slightly, Tyler continued.

'Think what it'll do to our little town. Can you imagine some faceless owner, sitting in his fancy boardroom in London, giving a second thought to what happens to this place? They'll pollute our river, poison our air and build on whatever land they want if it means turning a profit.'

He was pleased to see that his words were causing a stir. Some of the crowd were muttering angrily while others had started a chant, which Tyler joined in with on the megaphone. The abattoir was in a small industrial estate, and some of the other warehouse doors had opened, the interest of their occupants piqued.

The noise suddenly died down as two sleek, black cars turned the corner of the road and pulled up on the kerb outside the gate.

Some of the crowd decided that now was the time to leave, their nerve deserting them, not wanting to be spotted by one of the McNulty brothers. The owners of the abattoir had a fearsome reputation.

As the engines died, the two brothers emerged from one of the cars. Kevin McNulty was the eldest. His wiry, prematurely grey hair was complemented with a matching moustache and his alert eyes were presided over by a slab of a forehead. He was well over six foot, though stocky.

Ron, the younger brother, was different in almost every way. His angular jaw was coated in designer stubble and his hair carefully gelled to the side. Though much shorter than his brother, his muscular frame was evident under his perfectly cut three-piece suit. He may have had the face, but Kevin had the brains.

The brothers noticed the protesters chained to their fence at the same time. Ron's eyes narrowed, while Kevin gave a playful laugh, trying to make light of the situation for their guest, who had just emerged from the second car.

'I thought you said there wouldn't be any bother,' the man said in a Cockney accent, as he approached the brothers.

'This?' Kevin said, motioning to the blocked gate. 'This is no bother. Nothing to worry about. Sure, why don't you head back to the hotel for a while and we'll sort this? We'll give you a bell when we're ready to start the tour.'

The Englishman nodded curtly and returned to his car, which took off as soon as he had closed the door. The McNultys watched it disappear around the corner before shooing the crowd. Most, including some of the protesters holding the placards, made the smart decision to vacate the vicinity.

When the area was mostly empty, the McNultys advanced towards the gate. Tyler could feel the sweat running down his back, though he tried to appear confident as the two men stopped in front of him.

'These hippies,' Ron said, pointing at the protesters chained to the fence, 'are a bit of an annoyance. But *you* are blocking the gate. That makes you, and you alone, the object of our attention.'

'Meat is murder!' shouted Tyler, though with no audience, save for his fellow protesters, the words seemed to lack any substance.

Kevin sniggered.

'Your little stunt didn't go down well with Mr Jones. He is a man who is very conscious of public perception. In fact, if we don't show him around this afternoon, the deal could be off.'

'Good,' spat Tyler.

Ron's face reddened and he nodded to his elder brother who delivered a hefty punch to Tyler's midriff with one of his ham-sized fists. Tyler gasped for air as pain flared through his body.

'Now,' said Ron, addressing the rest of the group. 'Who's going to make the smart decision and leave?'

Most of the protester's hands shot up. No one wanted to be on the receiving end of a McNulty fist.

'You lot are smarter than you look, which isn't saying much,' Ron laughed, before turning to Tyler. 'And what about you?'

Still fighting to pull air into his lungs, Tyler summoned enough saliva to spit into Ron's face.

The brother pulled away in disgust, using his tie to wipe the spit off his chin.

'You are going to bloody well pay for that,' he said.

As he swung his arm back in preparation for an almighty punch, the wail of sirens filled the air. A couple of police cars mounted the kerb and a number of uniformed officers rushed towards the scene.

'You just got very lucky,' Ron whispered. 'But your luck will run out.'

He moved towards Tyler like he was going to punch him, though stopped short and laughed when he cowered. Ron nodded at a police officer as he passed, and he and his brother walked away, back towards the car they'd arrived in. Tyler smirked as he watched them go.

Phase one had been a success.

Now, it was time to turn up the heat.

2

FEUER FREI!

ADAM WHYTE LIFTED the last of the tools out of his van and placed them carefully into his lock up. Since moving into his own place, he didn't have the space to keep all of his gardening tools, so had rented a small storage unit nearby.

Though it was a small thing, it made him feel that bit more professional. Six months ago, he had been happy to lie about on the sofa all day, alternating games of FIFA with episode after episode of Sherlock and asking his mum to make him sandwiches for lunch.

All that had changed when he and his friend, Colin McLaughlin, had inadvertently taken on the roles of amateur sleuths and had now helped solve two murder cases that the police had written off as accidents.

The feeling of pride he'd had at solving those cases had spurred him on to do something with his life. That something had turned out to be a garden maintenance business. It had started small; just him, his car, a lawnmower and a rickety trailer he'd managed to salvage from the dump.

Now, here he was, unloading tools from a van with his name and company logo on the side.

When he was sure that the van was empty, he pulled the roller door of the storage unit down and secured it with a heavy-duty padlock. He pulled at the handle and, content that it was secure, got in his van and started the engine.

The journey still felt odd.

He had only been living in his flat for the best part of three weeks and had found himself, more than once, driving in post-work autopilot towards the familiarity of his mum's house instead.

He navigated the quiet roads and pulled into the car park at the rear of his flat a few minutes later. Grabbing his bag from the passenger seat, he jumped out of the van and walked to the main door. He held it open for an elderly lady he didn't know, before climbing the stairs to the third floor and jamming the keys into the lock on his door.

His flat was on the small side, and sparsely furnished, but the rent was cheap and it offered a panoramic view of the town he'd lived in all his life. And what a view it was: during the day, a small town with narrow cobbled streets and pretty buildings, surrounded by lush green fields. Beyond that, an endless ocean stretched out like a turquoise carpet. At night, a blanket of inky blackness allowed galaxies of stars, lightyears away, to settle in for the night like old friends.

He threw his bag down beside the sofa in the living room and headed for the kitchen, only realising as he opened the fridge just how hungry he was.

He grabbed a ready meal and stuck it in the microwave, admonishing himself for being so unhealthy. Adam had always been weedy, no matter what he ate, but since turning his hand to the hard graft of his job, his body had started to change.

Muscles he didn't know the name of had started to announce themselves and even his best friend Colin, a regular gym-goer, was impressed with the results.

If I could only get the diet right, Adam thought as he pulled the piping hot, processed lasagne out of the microwave, passing it from hand to hand to avoid a scalding. He mentally added oven gloves to the list of things it would be handy to own.

He made his way back into the living room and sat at the dining table, flicking the television on. Scrolling through Netflix until he found what he was looking for, he grabbed his fork and tucked into his tomatoey meal.

As he finished, his phone rang.

'Hello,' he answered. 'Whyte's Gardening Services.'

'Do you have to answer your phone like that every time?' asked Colin on the other end of the line.

'You never know when a business opportunity is going to arrive.'

'Well, you should know that when it's my name on your display, I'm not calling for your services. Even if I had a garden, I wouldn't trust you with it.'

'What do you want?' Adam asked.

'FIFA?'

'Yep.'

TEN MINUTES LATER, Colin and Adam were sitting on the sofa, picking their teams.

Adam had met Colin at primary school and they had remained best friends for the ensuing twenty years. They'd seen each other at their best and at their worst, and were all the closer for it.

'How are the old folks doing?' Adam asked.

'They're all alright. Barry is scouring the paper every week, trying to find us leads to investigate,' Colin laughed.

Colin worked in the Stonebridge Retirement Home. Since solving the two murders they'd stumbled into investigating, the residents had come to view him as some sort of messiah and sworn protector. One of the residents, Barry, was actively trying to find him cases, even though Colin told him his investigating days were over.

'I don't think I could handle any more excitement,' Adam said.

'I don't think Stonebridge has any more to throw at us.'

'You say that, but did you hear what the hippies were up to?'

'Aye, I saw it on the news. Braver folk than me, going up against the McNulty brothers.'

'Brave? Stupid, more like!'

'Anyway, enough of the neighbourhood watch,' said Colin. 'Hurry up and pick your team.'

With teams picked and tactics sorted, the game began. The usual jibes were thrown back and forth and, with ten minutes on the clock, natural order was restored. Adam was 2-0 down.

As half-time approached, a bright flash followed by an almighty wall of noise from outside caught their attention. They paused the game and moved to the window.

'Looks like a fire,' Adam said.

'And a bloody big one,' Colin added.

'Shall we go and have a look?'

'We just talked about not getting involved in excitement...'

'It's just because you're 2-0 up, isn't it?'

Colin conceded that that might be part of it, along with the general area of where the fire was. It took Adam a few more minutes of arm-twisting to get him out of the flat and down the stairs.

By the time they'd driven there, the entrance to the industrial estate had been blocked off by an assortment of emergency vehicles.

From the road, Colin and Adam could see that a horde of firefighters were battling the blaze that was destroying the McNultys' abattoir, trying their best not to let the flames spread to the neighbouring buildings.

A black Audi skidded to a halt on the closed road and Ron McNulty got out. He ran to the police officer at the cordon and gesticulated wildly, pointing at his crumbling business. The chatter of the crowd prevented Colin and Adam hearing what he was saying, but he didn't look happy.

When another police officer came over, Ron held his hands up in a placating manner and took a few steps back, running his hands through his dark hair. A few minutes later, Kevin pulled up in his Honda and the two brothers retreated back from the police line and watched as their business disintegrated before their very eyes.

'You think the hippies have got anything to do with this?' Colin asked.

Adam shrugged his shoulders, hoping that for their own sake that they didn't.

3

THE AFTERMATH

COLIN RAN INTO the common room of the Stonebridge Retirement Home, his heart in his throat. From the adjoining office, he'd heard a huge commotion start and it had jolted him out of his chair—worst case scenario thoughts running through his head.

'What's the matter?' he asked Betty, who was sitting in the chair closest to the door.

'Just Barry having a tantrum,' she said, and Colin simultaneously laughed and breathed out a sigh of relief.

He walked over to the corner with the television in it and found Barry holding court, instructing everyone to look for the remote.

'What's with all the hubbub?' Colin asked.

Barry pointed to the television in way of explanation.

'I can't stand this bloody show with that idiot presenter talking to the machine like it's his mate. All the pleases and thank yous of the day. It's a bloody inanimate object!'

'He's just being polite,' Colin replied, struggling to keep the grin from his face. The *Tipping Point* complaints had become almost a daily occurrence.

'Polite to a bloody arcade machine!' Barry shouted, before realising that Colin was messing with him. 'Oh, ha ha.'

'You're too easy, Barry.'

With the remote found and the television turned off, quiet once again descended on the room. Barry grabbed a newspaper from the arm of the chair he'd been sitting on and followed Colin to the table that was commonly used for crafts but was currently unoccupied.

'What do you think about this?' Barry asked, handing the newspaper to Colin as they sat down.

Colin took the newspaper from him and scanned the front page. The headline was about the fire at the abattoir a few nights ago and a black and white photo of the blaze accompanied the piece.

'They've found a body,' Barry said, unable to keep the excitement out of his voice.

Colin folded the newspaper and set it down, knowing that Barry wouldn't give him peace to finish it.

'Oh yeah?' Colin said, trying to sound uninterested.

'Yes, indeed. It's that wee hippy fella who was the instigator of the protest.'

'Jesus,' Colin said. He knew Tyler Love from school, having been in the orchestra together, though he'd had been a few years younger than Colin. 'Have they arrested anyone?'

'Nope. And it doesn't look like they're going to either. They think he snuck in and started the fire himself. That it got out of hand quicker than expected and he couldn't escape in time.'

Colin hadn't been expecting that answer. He'd heard about the protest and had fully expected the McNultys to take some sort of revenge. Had the police got it wrong?

He glanced at Barry and could see immediately what the old man was hoping for.

When Colin had played a part in solving the murder case of their friend, Daniel Costello, Barry had been excited. He'd hounded Colin for every smidgeon of detail he could get. A few months later, when Colin had been involved in another amateur investigation, Barry was convinced that he was some sort of Sherlock-style genius.

'What do you think, Columbo?' Barry asked.

'I think the police probably know what they're talking about,' Colin answered. 'And I don't fancy getting into it with Kevin and Ron McNulty.'

Barry looked disappointed, though he did acknowledge that the two brothers were bother through and through.

'It's a shame the youth of today have to resort to violence and fighting when there's a disagreement,' Kenneth said, having been eavesdropping on the conversation from a nearby armchair.

'The youth of today?' Barry repeated.

'Yes,' Kenneth nodded. 'Tit for tat arguing and escalation. Why can't they just talk to each other like civilised beings?'

Barry shot Colin a bemused look before answering.

'Ken, when you were a youth, you were in the RAF during World War Two. Did you try and engage Hitler in polite conversation?'

'Well, no...' Kenneth answered, knowing full well that Barry had him beaten.

'Did you fly over Hamburg in your spitfire and drop kind words out of your plane?'

'No.'

'No,' Barry repeated. 'You dropped bombs. Bombs that exploded and took buildings and lives with them. So, don't try and make out that the youth of today are doing something different to what we did. You don't have a leg to stand on.'

'I know,' Kenneth winked at Colin, pulling up the hem of his trousers to reveal a length of his metallic prosthetic leg. 'I haven't had a leg to stand on for thirty years.'

ACROSS TOWN, Adam pulled his van into the driveway of a potential new client. He gathered his notepad and his keys from the passenger seat, stuck a pencil behind his ear and jumped out. Glancing around, he couldn't help but notice the weed-free path, well maintained flower beds and manicured lawn.

Looks like whoever lives here is doing alright by themselves, he thought.

He walked up the path and pressed the doorbell. He could see a blurred figure grow larger through the frosted glass and a few seconds later, the door opened to reveal a short woman with dark, shoulder length hair. Her cheeks were rosy and her eyes puffy. She looked at him quizzically.

'Hi, I'm Adam Whyte. I'm here about the garden.'

The woman nodded at him, seemingly remembering that she had in fact called him earlier in the day, and opened the door wider. Adam suspected that she was leading him to the back garden, so was surprised when she turned into a cosy living room and sat down on a sofa.

Adam sat down on a stripy armchair and opened his notebook. He glanced over at the woman and saw that she was staring blankly at a spot on the wall above his head.

'What is it that you'd like help with?' Adam said, hoping to spur her into action. 'I can have a look at it and price it up for you.'

Still, she didn't speak. Adam snuck another glance at her. It looked like she was building the courage to say something, which struck him as odd.

'Mr Whyte…' she started.

'Adam, please,' he interrupted.

'Adam, my name is Jennifer Love and I've called you today to see if you would be willing to look into my son's death.'

Love.

She hadn't told him her surname on the phone earlier, otherwise he might've put two and two together. That explained the red eyes and her distracted manner. When he didn't speak, she continued.

'The police have decided that Tyler broke into the abattoir a few nights ago and set fire to the place, killing himself in the process… I just can't believe he's gone!'

At that, she burst into huge, wracking sobs and waved a hand at him. She got to her feet and left the room. A moment later, he heard another door close and supposed that she had gone to the bathroom.

Alone, Adam didn't know what to think. He'd known about the fire, obviously, but he hadn't known that a body had been found. And he certainly hadn't known that the police had announced that they believed that lead hippy, Tyler, was behind it.

Adam wished he paid more attention to the news.

Forewarned would've been forearmed.

A few minutes later, Jennifer re-emerged, mumbling apologies which Adam batted away.

'Listen,' she said, as she sat down again, this time with a steely glint in her eye. 'Tyler was a good boy. He joined The History Makers to make a difference. A peaceful one. There's no way he would've broken in and set fire to the place – that's not the type of lad he was.'

She fixed him with a hard stare.

'The police have got it wrong, and I want you to get to the bottom of it. To clear his name.'

With her spiel finished, she sunk back into her chair, her energy spent, fresh tears ready to fall.

Adam wanted to say no. He didn't know anyone connected to the case, so had no idea how to get a foot in. He especially didn't want to get tangled up in a case involving the McNulty brothers. However, looking at the shell of a woman mourning her son, he couldn't help but think of his own mother.

His resolve crumbled.

'I'll ask around, but I can't promise anything.'

'I'd start with the McNulty lads,' she said, and Adam nodded the kind of nod that stupid people do when they agree to do something stupid.

A half-smile touched her face as a single tear slipped down her cheek.

4

THE HISTORY MAKERS

LIKE MOST BAD ideas, this one was dreamed up in a pub.

The Railway was an equidistant stumble between Adam and Colin's new houses, and therefore was the sensible choice as their local. They'd been a handful of times, and, though they were by far the youngest, they enjoyed the convivial atmosphere, the choice of lagers and the fact that live sport was shown most nights on the big screen televisions.

Adam walked back from the bar carrying two pints of Harp. He set them carefully on the table and slid one towards Colin, before throwing a packet of peanuts his way too.

Colin eyed the salty snack suspiciously. Adam was a notorious tight-arse, so he must've had a good reason for trying to sweeten Colin up.

The two friends engaged in small talk, discussing everything from their jobs to football to the lack of a female presence in their lives. Colin was surprised to learn that Adam had joined an internet dating site, and was unsurprised to learn that, so far, there'd been little to no success.

'Let me look at your profile,' Colin said.

'Why?'

'Because I'm thinking of joining one myself and I want to see how it works,' Colin lied.

Adam sighed deeply and slipped his phone out of his pocket. He thumbed his passcode in and found the app, before handing the phone to Colin.

Colin took a few moments looking through the profile, scrutinising the claims made in the 'About Me' section and checking which photos he'd used.

'You had a bit of a photoshoot at work, did you?' said Colin, turning the phone so that Adam could see the picture he was talking about. 'You look like you're in some sort of perfume advert. All you need is a sailor suit!'

Colin howled with laughter as Adam snatched the phone off him, his face crimson.

'Who took that photo, anyway?'

'Mrs Jenkins,' Adam said. 'I told her it was for the website.'

'And she didn't wonder why you came with gelled hair and an ironed T-shirt to pull out some weeds from her garden?'

'Anyway,' Adam pushed on, as if he hadn't heard his friend, 'I wanted to let you know that I had a chat with Mrs Love today…'

'Tyler's mum?' Colin interrupted, suddenly serious.

'Yeah. She said she couldn't believe that the police were trying to pin the fire on her son; that he would never do that kind of thing.'

'He did chain himself to the building to try and stop a takeover.'

'Yeah, but there's chaining yourself to a building to make a point, and then there's arson.'

'You don't think he did it?' Colin asked.

Adam took a sip of his pint and considered the question. He could see both sides of the coin—Tyler could well have burned down the building to make sure his protest and subsequent beating were not in vain. Fires were unpredictable and the smoke could easily have overpowered him, in the middle of his act of pyromania.

On the other hand, Adam had seen first-hand how vehemently Tyler's mother believed that he was not the guilty party here. That he had died at someone else's hands.

'I don't know,' Adam admitted. 'But, I'd like to find out. What do you say—are you up for a bit of Sherlocking?'

Colin thought about it. The previous "cases" *had* been fun, but this was a different kettle of fish. This one could put them in the firing line of a pair of psychopathic brothers.

'Is she paying us?' Colin replied.

'She's just lost her son, have a little respect,' Adam said, as a huge burp escaped his lips.

'Fine, stop tugging on my heartstrings, will you? I'm in. Where do we start?'

'With the hippies,' said Adam.

THE NEXT MORNING, Colin and Adam walked down the middle of the town centre and turned left at the newly renovated Starbucks. It was on this cobbled side street that the unofficial headquarters of The History Makers resided.

'Don't you think that they'll be annoyed if two strangers turn up to a memorial service?' Colin asked.

'They're hippies,' Adam answered. 'Their whole schtick is spreading the love. Anyone asks, we're there to pay our tributes to Tyler. We'll have wheedled them with their own stupid life motto.'

'I don't think we should call them hippies to their faces,' Colin said, fixing Adam with a look that said this was a command rather than a suggestion.

'As long as they keep their new age BS to themselves, we're all good,' Adam replied.

Colin had been worrying about not knowing which house was the HQ, but he needn't have. Thick tendrils of bluish smoke drifted from the open windows, furnishing the street with the sweet, piney smell synonymous with weed.

A man wearing green bell-bottomed trousers and a fluffy vest with no T-shirt underneath it approached the house from the opposite direction. He nodded at Adam and Colin as he pushed the door open gently and disappeared into the wall of smoke. It reminded Colin of the Stars In Their Eyes set.

'Tonight, Matthew, I'm going to be...' he started

'Stoned, against my will, by the looks of things,' Adam interrupted, as he followed the man wearing a vest into the house with a scowl.

A narrow corridor, plastered with posters of cannabis leaves and other drug paraphernalia, led to a small living room and an even smaller kitchen. As they made their way down the hallway, Adam wondered if one of the group owned the house or if they were renting. If it was the latter, the landlord would be furious with the state of the place.

They poked their heads in the living room, where a small rave seemed to be underway. Though the hour hand hadn't yet reached eleven o'clock in the morning, every single person in the room was holding a bottle of something alcoholic and dancing along to the thumping bass and chipmunk vocals being spewed out by a speaker in the corner of the room.

'We're not going to get much sense out of anyone in there,' Adam shouted over the thrum of the music.

They walked further down the hall and entered the kitchen. The atmosphere in here was much more subdued. Pictures of Tyler adorned the walls and a few unusually dressed people sat around on the rickety dining chairs, crying and swapping stories.

'Hi,' one of them said, rising from his seat to greet Adam and Colin, arm outstretched.

They both shook hands with the man who had introduced himself as Jay.

'Would you like to write down a memory?'

'A what?' Adam asked.

Jay motioned to the square dining table. On it was a small plastic box, a pile of paper and a few biros.

'We're collecting memories from everyone here. Their favourite memory of Tyler. We very much wanted today to be a celebration of his life, rather than something downbeat. He would've hated that.'

'That explains the disco next door, then,' Adam said.

'Yeah. I think...' Jay trailed off. 'I think maybe that's a step too far.'

'You think?' Adam laughed.

'Who organised this?' Colin asked, giving Adam a death stare. The full Paddington.

'Well, I thought it would be a nice idea to commemorate his life with a memorial service here. Tyler was my best friend, so I mostly took charge. The memory thing was my big idea. Willow took it upon herself to organise the rave…' Jay said, casting an angry glance at the wall that divided the living room and kitchen.

'Who's Willow?'

'Our new leader, I guess. She was second in command to Tyler, but now that he's gone…' Jay dabbed at his eyes. 'Now that he's gone, Willow is in charge.'

'Is she in there?'

'Yeah, you can't miss her. She's got bright pink hair.'

'Of course she does,' Adam sighed.

They thanked Jay for his time and left the kitchen, making their way back into the living room. As Jay said, Willow was pretty easy to find. She was standing by the open window; eyes closed, a joint gripped between her lips as she swayed along to the music.

'She looks like she really misses him,' Adam said, noticing the smile on Willow's face.

Adam made to move but Colin put an arm across the door.

'I've got this,' he mouthed, noticing his friend's mounting annoyance.

5

AN UNWEEPING WILLOW

ADAM AND COLIN followed Willow up the stairs, away from the droning bass, trying not to look at her exposed G-string. She walked the length of the landing and wordlessly disappeared through the door at the end.

Adam shot Colin a confused look, which he answered with a shrug of his shoulders. Were they supposed to follow her in?

Thankfully, their confusion was short lived as Willow appeared in the doorway and beckoned them in with a flick of a finger. Adam pushed Colin in the back, gently, ushering him towards the door.

If Adam had been asked to sketch what he thought the inside of Willow's room looked like, he would've got about 90% right.

A couple of wicker peace signs dangled from nails above the headboard of her bed. Posters with drug puns such as "Don't drink and drive, smoke and fly" were stuck up on the other walls and on a desk facing the window, an overflowing ashtray sat alongside an old typewriter. Net curtains were being pushed into the room like holey ghosts by a gentle breeze coming through the open window.

Willow walked over to the desk and grabbed a cardboard packet, from which she pulled a single cigarette. She pushed some of the other things on the messy surface out of the way, searching for something.

'Lighter?' Colin said. He'd taken it off one of the care home residents earlier when they were threatening to light a recent prime minister's book on fire.

Willow looked at the translucent orange rectangle with disgust.

'Single use plastic?' she said, scornfully. 'No thanks.'

She eventually found the box of matches, and pulled one out, striking the stick along the side.

'Yeah, because cutting down trees to make matchsticks is so much better for the environment,' Adam muttered, though not loud enough for Willow to hear.

Smoking cigarette in hand, Willow crossed the room and sat down on the bed. She shifted backwards so that her back was against the wall, pulling her bare feet underneath her.

'I don't make a habit of letting two lads I don't know into my room,' she smiled. 'What can I do for you?'

'We were wondering if we could ask a few questions about Tyler?'

'Are you from the police?'

'No,' Colin said. 'The police have already said that Tyler's death was an accident.'

'So, you're what…? Private investigators?'

'Like I said, we just want to ask a few questions. We knew Tyler from school and him starting a fire and burning a business to the ground doesn't sound like something in his wheelhouse.'

'We were wondering if you could tell us anything about what happened that night at the abattoir,' elaborated Adam.

Willow tipped some ash into the glass ashtray and looked at them without expression.

'Well, I wasn't there, so I couldn't possibly know. I read in the paper that the police believe Tyler started the fire and then got himself trapped and died from smoke inhalation.'

'And does that sound plausible?'

'To be honest, yes. Truthfully, we didn't see eye to eye. The History Makers started as a group for good. We wanted to draw attention to things like climate change and show the town how little changes could make massive differences. When Tyler joined, he sort of assumed the leadership role and took us in a different direction.'

'What direction?'

'More… extreme. Like the protest that happened on the afternoon of his death. A couple of months ago, something like that would never have happened. He kept pushing and pushing us to show how much we wanted things to change.'

'He sounds… assertive,' Colin said, hoping that his apparent disapproval at Tyler's methods would keep Willow talking.

'Intimidating was more like it,' Willow said, extinguishing the cigarette in the ashtray. 'If you didn't do what he said, he belittled you in front of the group. He made out that no one cared as much as he did.'

'Sounds like a dick,' Adam chimed in.

'I never want to speak ill of the dead,' Willow replied. 'But he could be a dick. I mean, look at how he treated his girlfriend.'

'What do you mean?' Colin asked.

Willow's eyes widened as if she realised that she had started down a path she didn't want to continue. She took a few metaphorical steps back.

'Like I say, I don't want to speak ill of the dead. All I'll say is that he wasn't well liked.'

'By who?'

'By most of the group, but especially Ocean.'

Colin could see Adam struggling to keep a sarcastic comment under wraps, so barrelled straight in with another question.

'What happened after the protest at McNulty's Meats?'

'Well, those nutters who own the place turned up and gave us a chance to leave. Most of us did. I care about the environment, but I also care for my own safety. We got unchained from the fence, but Tyler stayed. We watched him take a punch or two before the police turned up. Before they could get to the gate, the brother who fancies himself whispered something in Tyler's ear.'

'Did Tyler say what?'

'No. After the protest we came back here. Tyler was fuming. He accused us all of wimping out on him, of selling him out. He trashed the kitchen, kept telling us how much we'd let him down. But he would've done the same to anyone of us. Tyler only ever looked out for Tyler.'

She rose from the bed and retrieved another cigarette from the desk, before retaking her spot against the wall.

'Do you think he lit the place on fire?'

'Well, he did say that he was going to pay them back for punching him. Once we'd managed to calm him down a bit, he sat in the front room, muttering to himself and getting himself worked up again. He left in the early evening without a word to anyone, never to be seen again.'

'And he didn't tell you what his payback was?' Colin asked.

Willow shook her head, causing ash to cover a section of the colourful duvet.

'He didn't tell me, but Helena went after him.' She looked up at the two blank faces. 'Helena was Tyler's girlfriend.'

'What happened when Tyler left?'

'To be honest, the rest of us saw the protest as a massive success. The English guy who is buying the factory left looking disappointed and the McNutters were furious, which meant we'd struck a nerve. We had a party to celebrate. Later, we saw on Twitter that the McNulty's Meats factory was on fire and we put two and two together.'

'Was anyone missing from the party?' Adam asked.

Willow squashed out the second cigarette and scratched at her fluorescent hair absent-mindedly. Finally, she nodded her head.

'Not everyone stuck around. It had been a long day and some people went home not long after Tyler left, but there's no way I could remember who was there and who wasn't.'

'You mentioned Ocean wasn't a fan of Tyler's…'

'You can say that again,' she interrupted with a snigger.

'Was she at the party?' Adam finished.

'Ocean is a guy,' Willow said. 'And, like I said, I can't be sure who was there. There were… substances being passed around, you know?'

'We'd quite like a chat with him. Is he here?'

'No,' she said, shaking her head. 'He's working.'

'Where?'

'At the Stonebridge Organic Food Store.'

'The *what?*' Adam exclaimed. He'd never heard of such a shop in his town.

Willow stood up, and made for the door.

'Can I go back to the memorial service now?' she asked.

Adam took in what she was wearing. Leopard print leggings and a black Slayer T-shirt; on the front of which a snake crawled out of a skull's empty eye sockets.

'Is that appropriate dress for a memorial service?' Adam asked.

Willow shrugged.

'At least I'm here… that's more than can be said for Helena.'

She raised her eyebrows suggestively before leaving the room, leaving Adam and Colin to mull over what they'd just uncovered.

6

AN OCEAN OF (UN)CALM

COLIN AND ADAM slipped down the stairs and left the house without another word to anyone. Any fresh air there'd been in the house had been pushed out by a heavy haze of green. Adam was spluttering as he crossed the threshold, though Colin was convinced it was for show.

'It's hardly Burning Man,' he said, 'chill out.'

'Chill out?' Adam coughed. 'Is that supposed to be funny? I'm so chilled out, against my will I might add, that my face is drooping.'

'That's just your jowls flapping from all the junk food.'

They ceased talking as Adam began lightly slapping his cheeks. Colin rolled his eyes and led them in the direction of what Adam called the "wrong" part of town.

Usually, the "wrong" part of a town or city would denote some sort of clear and present danger; the heart of the gangland territories, perhaps, or old sectarians doling out weapons to the new brigade in the hope of reigniting the dark days of the Troubles.

According to Adam, the wrong end of Stonebridge was worse.

To the casual observer turning into the offending street, the cause of Adam's chagrin might not be immediately obvious. It looked like any other street in the town. But, if Adam were to take you on a tour of his dislikes, he'd point you to Zen, the new age shop with a window display littered with crystals, glass skulls and tarot cards. Competing smells of incense drifted out through the bottom of the door, causing the street to stink of wood, flowers and spices.

Further along, a vegan café offered rabbit food to humans for a premium and, beside it, a clothes shop as dark as a nightclub catered for those who dared to dress differently.

Adam was all for people showing their personality through what they chose to wear (up to a point), but this was ridiculous. Opposite the boutique was the store they were here for.

A bell sounded as they pushed through the door. The lady on the till looked up from her magazine, smiled and offered her assistance. They assured her they were just here to browse, and she resumed her reading.

The shop wasn't very big and was bisected by a line of shelving. The smells of various vitamins and treatments mixed in the air, causing the room to smell a bit like a pet shop. Colin was going to mention this to Adam, though stopped himself in time. He needn't add more fuel to the fire.

At the back of the shop, a door flapped open and a man backed through it, carrying a stack of boxes. He lowered them to the ground and kneeled beside them, ready to start filling the shelves with their contents. Before he could start, Colin approached him.

'Excuse me, are you Ocean?'

The man pushed his dreadlocked hair out of his eyes and looked up at Colin.

'Yes, dude. How can I help you?'

Colin briefly explained who they were and what they were doing. When he finished, Ocean nodded once.

'I have a break in ten minutes. I was planning on eating in Renew, so if you want to nip across and grab a table, I'll meet you there.'

Colin thanked him, and he and Adam left the shop. As soon as they were outside, Adam's moaning began about the choice of eatery. A small smirk crept onto Colin's face, though he managed to hide it from his friend.

ADAM SIGHED AND picked up a menu, resigned to the fact that he was actually going to have to eat something. He didn't know how long Ocean would stay, but his stomach was already growling and he didn't think he could make it until they were finished their chat.

'There's nothing on here,' he muttered, after a minute.

'There's a sausage wrap.'

'Yeah, but the sausages aren't sausages, are they? They're Linda McCartney's idea of what a sausage is. And there's probably no gluten in the bread, which is the best bit.'

'You can't possibly know that gluten is the best bit of bread,' Colin replied, but this simply served to irritate Adam further.

His tirade against the café was stopped by the opening of the door and the appearance of Ocean. He was a hulking great figure; tall and muscular with dreadlocks dyed a light blue. A thick, dark beard covered the lower half of his face but, despite his intimidating size, his green eyes radiated a warmness. He seemed a walking contradiction—he *could* crush you, but wouldn't enjoy doing it.

'Alright,' he said, sliding into the booth beside Adam.

They both nodded their alright-ness as a waitress appeared.

'Hi Ocean. The usual?' she said.

Ocean nodded his assent and she turned to the two vegan noobs.

'What would you suggest?' Colin asked.

'The falafel wrap is really nice,' she replied.

Colin took her suggestion and added a glass of apple juice, while Adam succumbed to the call of fake sausages, though he still didn't look pleased.

'Does the orange juice have bits in it?' he asked.

'It's freshly squeezed, so yes,' she replied, as though this was a selling point.

'Course it does,' Adam muttered under his breath, before adding a glass of tap water to his order. The waitress smiled at them and touched Ocean lightly on the shoulder before turning and heading back towards the kitchen.

'How can I help you?' Ocean asked, now that they were alone.

'To be straight up, we've been asked to look into what happened to Tyler.'

'The police said he burned a business to the ground and killed himself in the process. Knowing Tyler as I do, or did, I'd say that sits perfectly well within the realms of possibility.'

'You weren't a fan?'

'Not overly, no. We both went to the same secondary school and he made my life miserable. He picked on me for my appearance, spreading rumours about my sexuality, that kind of thing. Things that matter a hell of a lot to a teenage boy who is trying to work out who he is.'

'That's tough. Sorry man,' Adam said.

'Thanks. I still get looked at for my hair, or for what I wear, but I don't care now. I'm older and I'm more confident, but those teenage years are hard enough with the devils on your shoulders, let alone having one in the flesh, taunting you daily.'

'So, how did you end up getting involved in the group?'

'Me? A few like-minded individuals figured Stonebridge needed a kickstart. So, we formed the group with the hope of showing the town, peacefully, that small changes can make big differences. We planned on leafleting and things like that. Non-invasive, not preachy, but just something, anything to try and help the planet.'

The food arrived as he finished speaking. The same waitress set the plates and drinks softly on the tabletop, before drifting out of sight again. For a few minutes, they ate in silence. Adam took a nibble from the corner of his sausage wrap and was pleasantly surprised by the burst of flavour.

He tried not to let it show on his face, though. If Colin caught sight of any hint of enjoyment, he'd never hear the end of it.

When the food had been seen to (Adam left a small bit on his plate just to make it look like he hadn't enjoyed it as much as he actually had) the questioning resumed.

'How did Tyler come to be involved then?' Adam asked.

'In his usual way. He caught wind of what we were doing and asked if he could help out. If I'd been there, I would've told him to do one. But, he was invited in and before we knew it, he'd assumed command and was making plans.'

'What kind of plans?'

'Plans that involved pushing the boundaries. Exactly what we had decided the group wouldn't be doing when we formed it. Like I said, we never wanted to ram our stuff down people's throats. But Tyler did, followed by a kick up the arse for good measure. The guy was a mercenary. He'd done this before with another group in the town, and they had the good sense to kick him out. Their leader is a scary bloke, though. We were all too nice to Tyler.'

Adam wrote the name of the group down in his phone with a reminder to look them up when he got home. Perhaps Tyler had done something awful in his previous group and the frightening leader had bided his time, choosing fire as a means of revenge.

'What about Helena?' asked Colin.

'She tagged along with Tyler, but you could tell her heart wasn't in it. It was like he was forcing her to be there.'

'Were they happy together?'

'Couldn't tell you, man. I tried to take as little notice of him as possible. Might be worth having a chat with her, though. He might've confided his plans to her. He didn't tell us diddly squat unless he was bossing us around.'

Ocean checked his watch and told them his lunch break was almost over. They slipped out of the booth and Adam told them he'd pay for lunch. Colin and Ocean walked outside, where the latter lit a roll-up cigarette.

Adam waited by the table and paid the waitress when she reappeared. He cast a conspiratorial glance over his shoulder, to make sure Colin hadn't sneaked in. When he saw that the coast was clear, he asked her a question.

'Do you do deliveries?'

7

A FURRY FRIEND

ADAM SPENT THE evening on the sofa. He'd finished some outstanding invoices for some of the council work he'd undertaken last month, and now came the really challenging part—getting them to pay.

Once the tedium of spreadsheets was done with, he stowed his laptop on the shelf under the coffee table and started the PlayStation. He navigated to Netflix and selected an episode of Peep Show he'd seen a billion times before. He only needed it on in the background, as he had another task to complete. This one, purely recreational.

He pulled out his phone and searched for information on the group Ocean had told them about earlier that day. It seems Stonebridge was fast becoming a political hotspot. The History Makers were campaigning for climate change and to stop capitalism, while rival group (if there could be rivals in trying to right the world's wrongs) Turn Back the Clock wanted to see less plastic in the seas.

He logged into Facebook and searched for this new group. It didn't take long to find their page.

Their mission statement was spelled out in the "About Me" section and there were a number of pictures showing a ragtag bunch at various protests and demonstrations. They were mostly women his age, though a tall man with tattooed arms and a buzzcut appeared in a number of them, too.

Even in the photographs Adam could sense the authoritarian in him. His stance, his soulless stare into the camera lens, the way he seemed to gather the female members of the group around him like a harem.

Perhaps he was being unfair to the man, though Ocean had hinted that he wasn't a very pleasant fella.

He dug a little deeper into the group and found a name—Mickey Dooley. Adam wrote the name down and started typing a text to Colin to discuss next steps, when his phone rang.

It was his mum.

'What are you doing tomorrow?' she asked.

'Hello to you, too. I'm fine, thanks for asking. How are you?' he laughed.

'Sorry, I'm just a bit excited. Are you free tomorrow?'

He checked his diary and told her that he had to cut Mrs Morrison's grass at some stage, but he was flexible with the time.

'Can you be here for 9?' she asked.

'In the morning? What's got you so excited?'

'You'll find out tomorrow,' she said. 'See you bright and breezy.'

With that, she hung up. His mum's phone habits were becoming more and more like a master spy. She'd tell you very little but leave your appetite whet. Sometimes, she didn't even say goodbye.

Adam wasn't fond of surprises and was dying to know what had got her knickers in a twist. He considered phoning her back, but knew she was like a steel trap when she wanted to be. Instead, he threw his phone to the other end of the sofa, sank back against the plump pillow and tried to take his mind of the many mysteries in his life by watching the finest comedy show ever committed to film.

WHEN ADAM PULLED up onto his mum's driveway the next morning, she was peering out from the window. Despite being a few minutes early, she had a scowl on her face.

Before he could undo his seatbelt, she was locking the front door behind her and making her way to the passenger side of his Clio.

'What kept you?' she asked, as she sat down beside him.

'What are you on about? It's not even nine yet.'

'It was by my clock. Anyway, let's not bicker. Guess where you are taking me?'

'I didn't know I was taking you anywhere.'

'Guess!' she said.

'The library?'

'Nope.'

'Stonebridge Retirement Home?'

'I don't know anyone there,' she replied, confused.

'I didn't say for visiting,' laughed Adam. 'I meant to get yourself a room!'

She slapped him playfully on the arm.

'We're going to the Dog's Trust! I'm getting a puppy!'

'Why?'

'Well, since you moved out, the house has been very quiet. I plod around on my own and last night, I saw an advert for this place and thought it would be nice to have a bit of company.'

Adam felt a pang of guilt as he thought of his mum being lonely without him. Perhaps a dog was a good idea.

He reversed out of the drive and asked his mum to type the postcode of where they were going into the sat nav. It had been a week or so since he'd seen his mum, and in between the robotic voice giving directions, they caught up. Adam told her about his busy gardening schedule and she told him about volunteering at the soup kitchen. His mum was just steering the conversation towards girls when a sign for their destination spared him having to tell her that there was nothing to tell.

They parked up and got out. A narrow gravel path led them up a small ridge towards the building. Barks and excited yelps could be heard before they'd even stepped foot inside.

The interior of the building was bright and welcoming. Smiling staff carrying bags of dog food strode with purpose towards the cacophony of woofs. It must've been breakfast time for the pooches.

A woman walked towards them and wanted to know if they needed help. Adam's mum explained their purpose here and the woman gave them both a rundown on how the adoption process worked. She showed them the way to the doggy showroom and left them with a promise that she'd be nearby if they needed her.

The sight that greeted them was both beautiful and sad. The far wall of the room was divided into eight small sections, each separated by a thin sheet of wood. Inside each section was a dog, waiting for someone to take them home.

Some were pacing around like a prisoner stomping the yard; some dashed this way and that, excited by the arrival of new humans while some simply lay in their beds, unfazed by the interest. Most were barking, as if trying to pull the attention of the visitors their way.

Adam and his mum strolled up and down the line, looking through the glass and reading the information that had been Blu-tacked to each partition. Adam could tell what his mum was thinking—she was wishing she could take every single one of them home. Probably would've done if he hadn't been here to keep her right.

At the end of the line, a little Shih Tzu caught her eye. A hair bobble kept its long hair out of its large, round eyes. It sniffed at the glass before putting one paw against it.

His mum instinctively reached out a hand and the deal was sealed.

The staff member from before must've been watching, as she came rushing over, delivering facts about the little dog. In a matter of minutes, they were outside watching her attach a lead to the dog's collar. She handed it to Adam's mum with a smile.

Adam and his mum circled the garden. The dog trotted along beside them, looking up every now and again as if to make sure this was actually happening. Adam's mum beamed the whole time and talked to the little hound in the way a new mother might talk to her new born. When the member of staff reappeared, it was to find that the dog was coming home with them.

They went inside and sorted the paperwork, arranging for a house visit the next day, just to make sure the dog was going home to a safe and secure home.

'You said his name was Daffodil?' Adam's mum said.

'Yeah, but he's young enough that if you wanted to change it, you could. He's a clever wee boy and he'll soon get used to something else.'

They bade farewell and Adam and his mum walked back to the car. She was fizzing with excitement.

'I can't wait to get him home with me. What do you think we should call him?'

Adam considered this while his mum spouted many different suggestions, ranging from musicians, to soap stars and everything in between.

'What's the guy's name from that Lord of The Rings thing you used to watch? They had some great names,' she said. 'Short fella. Starts with a D.'

'Umm…'

'Dildo!' she shouted suddenly. 'Is that it?'

Adam nearly crashed the car.

'Bilbo, mum. You definitely mean Bilbo.'

He quickly suggested more names, keen not to let her have Bilbo. He didn't want his subconscious to connect the poor dog with a sex toy every time he saw it. The little guy had been through enough already.

Adam spotted a petrol station, and pulled in to fill his tank. His mum told him that she would pay for it, and he tried to argue but it was like trying to take a restaurant bill off Mrs Doyle.

She disappeared into the shop and emerged a few minutes later, carrying the Stonebridge Chronicle under her arm. She got into the car and they pulled away from the pump. Adam glanced across at the paper draped over her knee and the headline caught his eye.

'What's that about mum?' he asked

She scanned the story briefly before replying.

'That company that were going to buy out the McNultys have found a new seller.'

'Does it say who?'

'You know I can't read in the car. It makes me feel sick.'

Adam considered this. Why was this English conglomerate so determined to set up camp in their small coastal town?

8

PLANS

'IT'S OPEN,' Adam shouted, in reply to the three knocks on the door. The handle turned in a ghostly fashion and the door opened, allowing Colin to enter. He walked down the short corridor and, upon reaching the living room, fell onto the sofa.

'I'm shattered today,' he said. 'The retirement home is getting a bit of a refurbishment and it's like bloody Piccadilly Circus!'

'Do you have to go back?'

'Aye, I only have an hour for lunch. What was so urgent?'

Adam explained about the newspaper article.

'Do you reckon it's Tanners?' Colin asked.

'Must be,' Adam replied. 'The article is vague, but it's the only other abattoir in town.'

Frank Tanner was the owner of Tanner's Meats. A very unimaginative name for a very unimaginative line of work. Founded in 1953 by Frank's father, Derek, it had been one of only two abattoirs in Stonebridge. When they were doing well enough, they'd expanded by opening a butcher's shop on the high street. On Saturdays, the queue for the freshest meat on the north coast wrapped around most of the town square.

This supposed success had not gone unnoticed. Like sharks drawn to spilled blood, the McNultys had sensed an opportunity to make a bit of money and really raised their game. Taking over from their father at the turn of the century, they'd poured serious investment into their business.

A business that was now in ruins.

'You think Frank had anything to do with the fire?' Colin asked.

'Maybe,' Adam nodded. 'I can imagine how he must've felt. He's been toiling away at the family business for all his life, and then these two McNulty yuppies wade in and are bought out for big money. It must sting a bit. Maybe he gets drunk one night and takes a torch to the place.'

'And kills Tyler by mistake.'

'Yeah. An accident. A dreadful one that he'll be put away for, but an accident nonetheless.'

'This is all conjecture at this point, though. We don't even know that it's Tanner at the centre of the new takeover,' Colin said.

Adam raised his eyebrows and Colin sensed the worst.

'I have a plan.'

Adam pulled his phone from his pocket and held up a picture. It showed the very professional website of the company who were behind the failed takeover of McNulty's.

'I'm going to pretend to be him,' Adam pointed at the boring looking man on the screen. 'Jonathan Jones. He was the one in charge of the buyout.'

'And say what?'

'Just you wait, mon frère.'

Adam found the number for Tanner's Meats and pressed dial, turning the phone to loudspeaker.

'Hello?' a man answered.

'O'wite mayte,' Adam started. 'It's John Jones 'ere. 'Ow you doin'?'

There was silence for a few seconds, that seemed to stretch out before them. Colin was about to curse his friend for ruining their chances of an in with Frank, when the man spoke.

'Mr Jones. Hello, I'm doing well, thank you. How are you?'

'A million dollars, pal. Listen, me secretary has only gone and lost some of the bladdy documents you sent across. Any chance you could fire 'em this way again?'

'Of course,' Frank said.

'And we're still on for next week?'

'Yes. I'll be there to greet you at the airport.'

'Cheers, pal. See you then,' said Adam, hanging up.

'What was that accent?' Colin asked.

'Cockney geezer, innit?'

'I don't think you'll be getting a part in EastEnders any time soon,' Colin laughed. 'But, good job. At least we know Tanner is the one set to make a fortune from the McNultys' misfortune.'

'Which means, he's just become our prime suspect.'

Colin nodded, rose from the sofa and walked towards the kitchen.

'Got anything to eat?' he asked, as he reached for the fridge door handle. Adam made a sort of strangled noise in return, that was mostly drowned out by the door opening.

'What did you say?' Colin asked.

'Nothing,' Adam answered, though he looked troubled.

Colin looked at him with a cocked eyebrow, before resuming his search for something to eat. His gaze settled upon a very out of place package on the bottom shelf. He smiled to himself, knowing that this branded, brown paper wrapped bundle was the source of Adam's reluctance to let him in the fridge.

'After all your moaning about the vegan café…' Colin said.

He shook his head in mock disappointment as he threw the offending packet of facon onto the kitchen worktop.

'Vegetarian bacon. Really?'

9

HEY MICKEY, YOU'RE SO FINE

IN THE CENTRE of town, just outside the Presbyterian church on the main street, a small crowd had gathered. It was mostly made up of teenagers, some dressed in Topman's uniform of skinny jeans and plain T-shirts, while the more out-there members of the group had pushed the boat out with some thrift-shop finery. Whatever their differences, they were united by one cause—listening to Mickey Dooley.

Colin watched from the doorway of a bookshop as the crowd nodded in agreement with the rhetoric that the man with the microphone was spouting. Disaffected youths, before his very eyes, were finding a cause to get behind. To find some meaning in their meandering teenage lives.

Who would've thought that the man shining that particular light would've been built like a tank with cropped hair like a soldier?

With a final bark urging the crowd to go forth and do right, he dispersed his disciples with a flick of the wrist. Some of the teens went left, some right. A couple started towards the local Starbucks. Evidently, sticking it to the man had no time constraints, and could wait until after their latte hit from a tax-evading multinational corporation.

Colin approached Mickey, who was busy packing up his microphone and portable speaker.

'Interesting stuff,' he said.

'Thanks, man,' Mickey replied. 'Are you interested in helping the environment?'

'As much as the next person. But, I'm actually here to talk to you about Tyler Love.'

Mickey looked momentarily wary, though his face quickly transformed itself into a mask of sadness.

'Poor Tyler,' he said. 'Horrible way to go.'

'I heard he used to be part of your group.'

'Well, firstly it's not my group, per se. Hierarchy breeds contempt and, as such, we instigated an egalitarian philosophy for Turn Back the Clock. We want everyone to be happy and willing to fight for a cause, so we subscribe to more democratic notions.'

'So, everyone is equal and you vote on ideas,' said Colin, trying to prise apart the political mumbo jumbo.

'Essentially, yes.'

'And, so, Tyler was once part of the group which you are also a member?'

'Yes, Tyler came to us a while back. As I said, we very much have an all-for-one type philosophy and so Tyler found ingratiating into the group… difficult.'

'Why?' Colin asked.

'Well, mainly because he wanted to be in control. If we said the sky was blue, he'd say it was green. Any vote that we did, he'd argue the outcome. He wanted to dictate, and we didn't let him.'

'What did he want, that you wouldn't do?' Colin asked.

'He wanted to adopt a more volatile practice than we had set out to use. He very much wanted to capture people's imaginations in the wrong way, often speaking about "big plans".'

'Like setting buildings on fire?'

Mickey gave a non-committal shrug.

'And so, you kicked him out?'

'Well, we uninvited him from the group and when he wouldn't accept, we had to be more direct?'

'Direct how?'

'Well, he and I had words.'

'And how did that go?'

'He gave me a black eye and damn well near shattered my skull. It was a cheap shot. He also smashed my car windows.'

'Jesus,' Colin said.

'Aye, I could've done with some of his divine intervention, to be fair.'

'Did you retaliate?'

'No, I didn't see the point. He'd already hurt me and trashed my car, if I'd goaded him further, who knows how it would've ended. I mean, I know I look handy, but I really deplore physical violence and am loathe to use it.'

Colin looked at his heavily tattooed, muscly arms and thought about the damage they could do if Mickey decided to free them. He also wondered if punching was off limits, but lighting a match wasn't. He didn't want to ask him outright, though.

'Do you think Tyler was capable of burning down a building? Colin asked, instead.

'Easily,' Mickey replied.

Colin thanked him for his time and started to walk away towards the car park, filing the conversation as inconclusive in his head. He thought the comment about hating physical violence was quite telling. Perhaps, after suffering at the hands of Tyler Love, he had simply bided his time until he could take some sort of revenge.

And that revenge had quickly spiralled out of control.

With these thoughts taking up most of his thinking space, it wasn't until he saw the sign for long defunct DVD rental shop that he realised that he'd walked in completely the wrong direction. Cursing himself, he was about to double back when his eyes fell onto a new shop.

The store, tucked between a bakery and a bookmaker, had recently been painted white and the slew of busy workmen suggested that time was of the essence in an attempt to get it open.

The front was anonymous, save for a pile of silver letters propped up against the wall, waiting to be fixed above the expanse of glass that would serve as a window for its wares, once the shop was open.

Colin was no countdown champion, but even he could work out that the jumble of letters would spell Tanner's once they had been correctly ordered.

He watched as a builder, covered in flecks of paint and dust, downed his drill just outside the door and took off his hi-vis jacket and helmet. He muttered something to another builder, who clapped him on the back and disappeared inside. The first builder walked in the direction of the café opposite.

Colin watched him go, before seizing the opportunity handed to him. Before anyone could notice what he was up to, he'd crossed the boundary and pulled the hard hat on, adjusting it so it covered as much of his face as possible. He shrugged the jacket on and stepped inside.

Colin didn't know much about butchers, but inside looked state of the art to him. Sloping silver display trays dominated the space, serving as a barrier between the area customers could wait in and where the butcher would work. The empty display, devoid of meat, looked strange. Weighing scales, knife racks and other paraphernalia filled the marble counters behind the display and a door on the back wall led to somewhere Colin couldn't see.

He imagined there was nothing to be gained by looking either.

One thing was certain, though. Tanner was already using the money from the takeover deal to expand his empire. Colin could only imagine how the McNultys were taking the news of their rival's windfall.

Perhaps Tanner *did* have something to do with the burning down of the McNultys' business. He was certainly profiting from it.

Colin reckoned it might be prudent to have a chat with the newly minted butcher.

He left the shop and set the hard hat and jacket where he had found them. He glanced up at the window of the café and saw the builder looking down at him, confusion creasing his wide face.

Colin took off in the other direction as quickly as he could. Since they were interviewing potential suspects in a possible murder enquiry, they were sure to make enemies and he didn't want to add an angry builder to the mix.

10

WHAT'S THE WORST THING I COULD SAY?

ADAM STOPPED MOWING the grass and wiped the sweat from his brow.

Summer was mostly a fanciful notion in Stonebridge. Usually, as the months that were tied to the season rolled around, talk turned excitedly to beach trips and outdoor activities.

The reality was that the sun would shine in a cloudless sky for about three days cumulatively, and the rest of the time was business as usual in Northern Ireland: heavy rain.

Today was one of the days where the sun beamed down and made everyone and everything seem happier. Mrs Young had been out not long ago to deliver him a glass of lemonade with the promise of a freshly baked cookie when he had finished his day's toil.

His work, however, had been interrupted by a ringing phone. He pulled his earphones out and looked at the unknown number that was flashing on his screen.

'Hello?' he answered.

'Is this Adam?'

He confirmed that it was whilst wracking his brains, trying to figure out if he's accidentally put his number onto his profile on the dating site. He didn't think he had.

'This is Helena. You messaged me on Facebook, asking me to get in touch with you.'

'Ah, I wasn't sure if you would. Thank you. Umm… I was wondering if you wouldn't mind me asking a few questions about Tyler.'

'Why?' she asked.

'Well, we're trying to find out what happened. His mum asked us to look into it.'

There was silence for a moment.

'I don't see the point in dragging all of that up again. It hurt too much telling the police what I knew first time around.'

He sensed she was about to hang up.

'Please,' he pleaded. 'Give me half an hour of your time and you'll never hear from me again.'

'Half an hour?' she repeated. 'That's more than most boys can promise.'

Adam was flustered by her flirty comment and mumbled something indistinctive. When she asked him to repeat what he'd said, he cleared his throat and tried to regain some composure.

They agreed to meet at Bar7 later that night.

'Don't be late,' she said, and then hung up before he could reply.

He sat down on Mrs Young's garden bench, his head spinning. Never mind the McNulty headcases, the hippies and the multinational corporations they were meddling with. It was Helena Bryer that was making him nervous.

He pocketed his phone, turned up the music and went back to work at double speed. He was going to need as much time to get ready as he could, if he wanted to impress Miss Bryer.

And he did want to impress her.

ADAM SAT AT a seat near the window in Bar7, overlooking the bustling promenade and, beyond that, the infinite sea.

Growing up, he'd sometimes been frustrated that all the action seemed to be confined to the capital, over an hour away. Bands he loved would never dare venture any further north than Belfast, so the only live music he'd been exposed to had been local bands playing tiny local venues.

Now, though, he realised just how lucky he was to live where he did. He'd finally recognised the beauty in the beaches, the ocean and the landmarks that tourists travelled thousands of miles to see.

His thoughts of his hometown were banished from his mind upon the arrival of Helena. Her dark, wavy hair spilled onto her shoulders and intelligent brown eyes scanned the room. She wore a strappy vest top with skinny jeans that stopped half way down her calf, exposing a small crescent moon tattoo just above her ankle.

Her eyes locked onto his and she gave a small wave, before starting towards him.

Adam could feel butterflies flutter in his stomach that had nothing to do with what he was about to ask her.

'Adam?' she asked, raising a hand hesitantly.

He nodded and, instead of shaking her hand like any normal person would, he grasped it lightly and raised it to his lips. He placed a delicate kiss on the back of her hand before the horror of the past few seconds had registered.

'I'm so sorry,' he stammered, practically hurling her own hand back at her. 'Uh, can I get you a drink?'

She laughed at his awkwardness and told him what she'd like. Adam excused himself, walked past the bar and into the toilets. He marched up to the sink, spun the handle on the tap and used his cupped hands to splash water onto his face, in the hope of regaining some composure.

When finished, he dabbed at his face with a paper towel and looked at himself in the mirror. He fiddled with his hair and ran a finger along his jaw, happy with the decision to shave off his scraggly beard before tonight's meeting. He looked good. But even at his best, he was still several leagues below Helena.

The momentary thought that flashed through his mind that she was now single, thanks to the death of her boyfriend, was laughable. Even if she wasn't in mourning, there was hardly a chance of romance there.

Delusions of grandeur, his granny would say.

He left the toilet feeling calmer. He stopped at the bar, ordered her a cocktail as well as a pint of Harp for himself, and then returned to the table.

He slid the cocktail in her direction and held his own glass aloft, which she clinked.

'Thanks for agreeing to meet me tonight,' he said.

'No problem. Sorry I was so reticent on the phone earlier. It's been hard, you know.'

Adam couldn't imagine what it would be like to lose a girlfriend in such tragic circumstances. Namely because he'd never had one. Still, he had to remind himself why he was here: she had been signposted by the hippies as a suspect. He couldn't let her good looks soften him.

'It must've been a very difficult time. I'll try to make my questions quick. Can you tell me about The History Makers?'

'They are a group of people who want to make a change.'

'And you are part of the group?'

'Was,' she corrected him. 'I only went because I was with Tyler. He dragged me along so that I would vote for whatever it was he wanted.'

'So, you weren't interested in their cause?'

'As much as the next person. Obviously, I care about the environment and would rather people recycled and drove electric cars, but going to weekly planning meetings on top of events was a wee bit overboard.'

'Sounds it,' Adam agreed.

'So, after what happened to Tyler, I haven't bothered anymore.'

Adam took a long sip of his pint as he tried to work out how to word the next question without sounding blasé about her ex-boyfriend's death. He set his glass down and licked some of the froth away from his lips.

'Can you tell me anything about the day of… the fire?'

At the mention of the fire, her face fell, and Adam's first thought was that he had ruined his chances of finding out more. His second was wondering if the look that had flickered across her features was one of guilt. She breathed out deeply, knocked the rest of her cocktail back in one go, and faced him again.

'We all went to the McNulty protest. It was Tyler's passion project. I think it was his way of showing the other members of the group that he had the balls to be head honcho. I mean, who else would go up against the Stonebridge Krays?'

She laughed, though it sounded empty.

'When that didn't quite go to plan, we all went back to HQ. He was fuming. At the McNultys, at the other group members and at himself. He'd shown weakness, you see? And so, he started mumbling to himself about showing everyone what he was really made of. Before anyone could calm him down or talk some sense into him, he'd gone.'

'What did you do?'

'I ran after him,' she replied. 'But, he told me that this was a one man mission and to run on home. We had a bit of a fight in the street, and then he left.'

'Was that unusual?'

'Fighting? No. It was quite a regular thing towards the end. We came very close to breaking up a load of times. I didn't like how much time he spent at the group, and he didn't like how much I moaned about it. One night, when he was drunk, he…'

She broke off, a sob escaping her.

'You don't have to tell me anything else,' Adam said, but she shook her head.

'No, it feels good to get it off my chest. He hit me—slapped me across the face. I told him that was it, but the next morning he came over with a bunch of flowers and apologised and, like an idiot, I fell for it.'

'I'm sorry to hear that,' Adam said, and considered placing a consoling hand on her bare arm, but instantly remembered the fumbling kiss at the start and thought better of any more unwanted contact. Instead, he said, 'can I ask one more question?'

She nodded.

'What did you do after your fight in the street?'

'I went home with my tail between my legs.'

'Home?'

'Yes,' she said, eyeing him suspiciously. 'I didn't have anything to do with what happened, if that's what you're thinking?'

Adam waved his hands in front of him, indicating that such a thought had never crossed his mind, when, in fact, that very idea was ringing sirens in his head right now.

When she offered to get the next round in, he convinced himself quite quickly that leaving now would look strange, and that he could use this time to acquire a bit of background info on her. Like a real private investigator would.

So, just like a real PI would, he accepted her offer and watched her make her way to the bar, along with every other set of male eyes in the place.

Another drink became a few and by the time they stumbled out at last orders, they were well acquainted. Adam had found out lots about her upbringing, her job and her interests and, in the process, developed a huge crush on her.

A crush on a possible murder suspect.

Just great.

11

MANFRED MANN

EVERY FIBRE IN Adam's being was currently dedicated to not throwing up inside Colin's car. If he did, he'd never hear the bloody end of it.

And, it wouldn't be a fair way to reply his friend's current kindness. When last night's "interview" with Helena had turned to serious drinking, he'd been forced to abandon his car. He and Helena had shared a taxi back to Stonebridge, though she'd gotten out at her own house, dashing any lewd hopes that had started whirling through Adam's drunken head.

Now, Colin was giving him a lift back to Portstewart to retrieve his car, though Adam was unsure if he was even under the limit yet. When he voiced this, Colin suggested they head for a fry up in The Atlantic. Even the thought of the smell of greasy food forced Adam to redouble his efforts in keeping last night's lager at bay.

When they reached the car park, Colin pulled into a space and they got out. They walked down the prom towards the café, Adam feeling very much like a wounded soldier, though receiving far less sympathy than he'd like.

They chose a table with a sea view and placed their orders (a full Ulster Fry for Colin and a slice of toast for Adam), before talk turned to where they were up to with the current case.

Colin told Adam all about his meeting with Mickey; how Tyler had physically assaulted him and then smashed his car up, just because he'd been asked to leave the group.

'So, there's definitely some motive there,' Adam said.

'Definitely,' Colin agreed. 'He claims he's not into physical violence but he's a scary-looking mofo, so I'm not sure I believe him. What about Helena?'

Adam told Colin what he'd learned; that Tyler had hit her, too. They foolishly had gotten back together, though were close to breaking up for good.

'Jesus,' Colin said, 'It's no wonder Tyler ended up the way he did. He was making enemies left, right and centre.'

'Yeah. So, we've got Willow who he pissed off by taking over the group; Ocean, who he pissed off by bullying at school and then taking over the group; Mickey, and Helena.'

'Don't forget the McNultys. He pretty much single-handedly stopped their business deal going through with his protest. Oh, and somehow Tanner benefits out of all this.'

Colin relayed the information about the new butcher shop in the middle of town.

'We need to start eliminating people,' Adam said, just as the breakfast came. 'What's next?'

'Well, I was speaking to my gran this morning and she was telling me about the McNultys' dad. Apparently, he's been looking for a retirement home. I thought I could go to the McNultys and pitch the home where I work, try that angle. If they see me as a friendly, they might let their guard down. And, more importantly, not batter me!'

'Good plan. How do grannies know so much?'

'I know,' Colin said, shovelling some soda bread into his mouth. 'It's like they have some sort of underground network for gossip.'

'I bet your gran would have this case sown up in no time at all. Maybe we should get her on board.'

'I don't think we could afford her. She'd bankrupt us on coffee alone.'

COLIN MADE HIS way up the street, the greasy food weighing heavily in his stomach, towards the McNultys' temporary office space. Their headquarters, which had been on the first floor of their warehouse, had obviously gone up in flames the night of the fire, so they had been forced into the centre of town.

In fact, their office space overlooked the shop currently being turned into Tanner's Butchers. Talk about adding insult to injury.

As Colin reached the office, he looked up to the first floor windows. The letters that had been painted on by the last owner, a tailor, were peeling and faded. But, this was not the reason for Colin's skyward glance.

It was the shouting.

Two male voices tumbled through the single-glazed window and out onto the street. Each response was upped a decibel until Colin was sure their argument could be heard at the other end of the town.

Suddenly, a loud bang sounded, presumably a door being slammed, followed by footsteps on uncarpeted stairs. A smartly dressed Ron McNulty emerged into the sunlight, his hair coiffed to perfection. He pulled a pair of sunglasses from his jacket pocket and put them on, glancing at Colin as he did so.

Colin watched him walk away, pulling a packet of cigarettes from a different pocket. Pushing Ron from his mind, Colin walked through the door and ascended the stairs, before rapping his knuckles on the flimsy door when he reached the top.

'It's open,' a voice called.

The door opened into a basic office. Two desks took up most of the space. The desk he assumed as Ron's was empty, save for a laptop that was charging, and a blue folder. Both items were positioned parallel to each other.

The other desk was messier, as if real work actually got done at it. Sheafs of paper jostled for position with binders and notebooks, rolls of receipts and a couple of mugs of gone-cold coffee.

Behind this desk sat Ron's older brother, Kevin; his grey hair falling onto his elongated forehead and his shirt sleeves rolled up against the heat.

'Who are you?' he said, without warmth.

Colin introduced himself, and told Kevin of the reason for his visit. He tried to sell the retirement home as genuinely as he could, explaining the benefits of assisted living and the activities laid on for the people who lived there. He passed a brochure across the table, which Kevin lifted and flicked through, stopping abruptly at the pricing page.

'Ah,' he said. 'Slight bump in the road there. Unfortunately, at the moment, myself and Ron are unable to fund this, as we are waiting for the insurance money to come through. I'm sure you are aware as to what happened.'

Colin nodded and mumbled his apologies.

'Unless you did it, you have nothing to apologise for. It was an act of arson by a small-time thug, and we may have missed out on the investment, but all shall come good. Sadly, our father's incarceration,' he flashed a small smile at the word, 'will have to wait until such times as our cash is flowing again.'

'Missed out?' Colin said, playing dumb.

'Yes, sadly it seems that Mr Tanner is rising from our ashes.'

Kevin raised his eyes towards the window, but didn't elaborate further. He stowed the brochure inside one of the desk's drawers and stood, offering his hand, seemingly in a manner that marked their meeting as over.

Colin shook it and left. As he neared the doorway that led back to the street, he heard someone speaking heatedly, apparently on the phone as the conversation was punctuated by silences.

Colin stayed listening for a minute, and was shocked by the anger in the man's voice. When the worry of being caught eavesdropping reached fever pitch, he made his way out onto the street. He was pleased to see that Ron McNulty's back was to him, and even more pleased when he caught the final words of the conversation before Ron replaced his phone into his trouser pocket and disappeared up the stairs Colin had just come down.

Colin hurried up the street and, when he was absolutely sure that he was out of earshot, phoned Adam who answered on the second ring.

The conversation didn't last long. Colin ordered Adam to meet him in town as soon as possible. Something was going down, tonight, and they needed to be there.

'What did he actually say?' Adam asked.

'Usual place. 6pm.'

'Which means?'

'Which means we have to follow him to wherever this usual place is, so get your arse into town. Now.'

12

A QUICK DETOUR

ADAM HUNG UP and checked the time on the dashboard. As ever, Colin was being a tad melodramatic—it wasn't even four o'clock yet. If he had to abandon his plan now, it'd be a while until he got round to it again, so he made the brave decision to ignore his best friend's urgency.

Instead, he climbed out of the car and walked up the driveway to the house Tyler Love had shared with his mum before his death.

He snuck a look through the net curtains as he passed the kitchen window, but could only make out his own reflection.

He made his way to the door and pressed the doorbell. It chimed a cheerful tune which felt horribly out of place, considering what he was here to do. As the tune faded out, he heard footsteps approaching and a few seconds later, he was face to face with Jennifer.

The saying "time heals all wounds" had clearly not been thought through enough. Perhaps, eventually, the passing of time may soothe Tyler's mother's grief, but here and now, it looked like she had aged decades since Adam had last seen her.

Dark bags hung heavily underneath bloodshot eyes and thin lines travelled down her face, as if the weight of the tears she'd shed had been so numerate that they'd carved narrow valleys into her cheeks. She tried, and failed, to give Adam a smile, and instead led him into the living room he'd sat in on his first visit here.

'Any updates?' she asked, as she sat down on the sofa.

'Not yet, I'm afraid,' he replied, and her shoulders slumped. 'But, we have spoken to a number of people and have some avenues we'd like to explore, so we're still working on it.'

He hated that he sounded like a character from a detective show, masking empty words with fancy phrasing, but giving it to her straight seemed worse somehow.

No, sorry. No progress yet aside from finding out that your son sounded like he was a bit of a prat to everyone, not to mention a woman beater and a thug.

Fancy phrasing would have to do at this stage.

'The reason I'm here is that I'd like to have a look around his room, if that's okay?'

'Why?' she asked.

'It's something that's worked before.'

He consciously left out the bit about hiding in a wardrobe like a voyeuristic Mr Tumnus while listening to a recent widow and her bit on the side have sex. Though he liked to think that it had been a maverick move, even he knew it sounded more like the behaviour of a sex pest. Not something the grieving mother sitting opposite him needed to hear right now.

Or anyone, ever, really.

If he could strike it from his own memory like the guy in Eternal Sunshine of the Spotless Mind, he would.

Pushing these thoughts from his brain, he realised that she was nodding. He listened to her directions and headed for the stairs, taking them two at a time. The flowery pattern underfoot reminded him of the carpet in his mum's house and a little knot of emotion formed in his throat when he thought of how she would handle losing him.

He resolved to put all ill-thought of Tyler to the back of his mind for the sake of Jennifer Love.

Upon reaching the top of the stairs, he turned left and took in the door in front of him. It was painted white, but had two slightly discoloured, sticky patches at about eye level, as if a poster or plaque had recently been taken down. The door was slightly ajar, giving it the air that the owner of the room had nipped out and never thought to close it fully one last time.

Adam pushed it open and was met with a tidy room. A bed took up the middle of the floor. A bookcase rested against one wall and a mahogany chest of drawers filled the other. A small television was mounted to the wall that faced the end of the bed. Adam imagined a buttock-shaped groove on the mattress, formed through countless hours of sitting playing FIFA.

Then, Adam remembered that he and Tyler were not cut from the same cloth. While Adam had been content to while away hours in front of the tele, Tyler had been out on the streets, fighting the good fight.

Or, if not "good", then at least fighting for something.

Adam didn't know what he was looking for particularly; perhaps he simply wanted to know a little more about Tyler in the hope that something might leap out at him.

He started by looking through the bedside cabinet, but nothing of note became apparent. It was mostly magazines; publications by Greenpeace, Planet Mindful and the like. He closed the drawer again and stood, looking around the room.

He searched through Tyler's clothes drawers, but aside from a few loose condoms in the sock compartment, again came away empty handed. He spun on the spot and his eyes settled on the book shelf.

It had five shelves altogether. The top four were dedicated to paperbacks; mostly crime, though interspersed with some YA fantasy. The bottom shelf, however, was filled with notebooks.

Adam crossed the room and got down on his hands and knees, pulling some of the spiral bound notebooks out onto the floor. His heart picked up its pace, and he wondered if the plan to ignite the McNultys' warehouse had been a plot weeks or months in the making.

When he'd spoken to the hippies, they'd suggested that he'd left the HQ that night seething, making it seem like the firebombing was a spur of the moment thing.

But what if they were wrong?

Adam flicked through page after page, aware that time was ticking on and Colin would be getting angrier by the second, so he skimmed faster. To his disappointment, the notebooks were mostly filled with journal entries about things that had happened, or plans for peaceful protests.

There was nothing to incriminate him.

Frustrated, Adam lifted the pile and shoved them back into the bottom shelf. The one at the end knocked against the wooden frame and fell out, opening as it did so, onto a bookmarked page Adam must've missed in his haste.

The page itself was unremarkable, but the item marking the page was certainly something. On it, was a scrawled mobile number and a little heart coloured-in black with biro.

Adam wondered if it was simply a remnant of when Tyler and Helena had first met, but surely he would just have typed her number into his phone's memory.

He pulled his phone from his pocket and found Helena's number, checking it against the one on the page to see if it matched.

It didn't.

He typed the number from the paper into his phone and was about to press the green button, when his ringtone erupted.

Colin.

'Where the hell are you?' he asked, as soon as Adam had answered.

'Keep your hair on, I'm two minutes away,' Adam lied, and hung up.

Making sure he had the number saved, he replaced the scrap of paper inside the notebook and set it back onto the bottom shelf. He cast one last rushed glance around the room, before hurrying down the stairs and saying a very brief goodbye to Jennifer.

He needed to find out who the phone number belonged to. It might be nothing, or it might be something.

However, he *had* to get to Colin in the next ten minutes. If he didn't, he might not be alive to guide the case to its conclusion.

With that thought in mind, he crossed the street in haste and wheelspun away from the kerb.

13

USUAL PLACE. 6PM.

COLIN THREW HIS phone onto the passenger seat in
frustration and sat back sharply, smacking his head a little too
hard on the headrest.

He assumed whatever Adam was up to was something to do
with the case. Or hoped so, anyway. With a solid gold lead in
the bag, he'd be very annoyed if Adam was doing something to
jeopardise all the hard work they'd put in so far.

He glanced at the clock again, for the third time that minute,
and sighed.

Colin had managed to find a spot to park his car that offered
a dual view of what he needed. He had an unhindered sight of
the main street, which allowed him to cast his beady eye over
the comings and goings of the McNultys' temporary office. Not
that there was much to see. Since Colin had left, Ron had re-
entered and there had been no further activity.

The spot also allowed him to keep his eye on the entrance to
the private car park that the row of shops used. At the first sight
of Ron's Audi departing, he'd be after him like a shot, with or
without Adam.

He looked at the clock, again. And swore, again.

Except, his curse word was cut short as something of note
was happening out on the street.

Frank Tanner, tall and broad-shouldered, stepped out of his
almost-finished butchers and looked up and down the street, as
if trying to ascertain if his shop was in a good place for passing
footfall.

Something a good businessman would have considered
before putting pen to paper on the deeds, thought Colin. Was

he simply taking in his empire? Or stalling on whatever he was about to do next?

In answer, he pulled a cigarette from behind his ear and shoved it into his mouth, before igniting the end of it with a disposable lighter. He took a deep suck in and exhaled a plume of smoke. When it cleared, Colin could see that his eyes were now fixed on the McNultys' office across the street.

Frank took a few more puffs before stubbing the cigarette out on top of a nearby bin and disposing of it. He marched across the street and disappeared through the doorway of his competitors.

Colin imagined the butcher bursting backwards through the upstairs window, shattered glass raining from the sky, bones breaking as Frank's body collided with the cobbles below.

It didn't take long for something to happen, though not quite the over-the-top imaginings going through Colin's mind.

Frank appeared first, emerging backwards. Initially, it looked like he was doing the moonwalk, which was a comic sight, until Ron appeared too. The McNulty brother was holding the other man by the scruff of his jacket, pushing him out of his office. They were exchanging words, and not kind words, judging by the disgusted faces of the little old ladies who happened to be passing at the wrong time.

Frank attempted to fight back, though that seemed to enrage Ron further. He shoved Frank up against the wall and delivered a fist to his gut, before releasing his grip. Frank dropped down the brickwork onto the floor, where he slumped over sideways, almost assuming the foetal position.

Ron shouted something inaudible to Colin, before retreating up the stairs and out of sight.

Frank lay for a little while longer, drawing a small crowd. Some crouched beside him, phones in hands, probably offering to phone the police, though the stricken man was shaking his head. In the end, he pulled himself to his feet and the crowd dispersed.

Frank cast an eye up the stairs, perhaps wondering if round two was worth pursuing. Evidently, he decided against it. Instead, he walked away, rubbing his stomach gingerly.

What had Colin just seen?

Did the McNultys believe Frank was behind the arson? And if he was, why would he go and visit them in their office? Surely, he would want to keep as much distance as humanly possible. Everyone knew what the psycho brothers were capable of.

Before he could make sense of the questions, the passenger door opened, and Colin jumped a foot in the air.

'What the hell?' he shouted.

'What's up with you?' Adam asked, as he slipped into the seat.

'Nothing, just…'

As he was about to explain what he'd just seen, the front end of a black Audi poked out of the car park. Using his mirror, Colin could see Ron's head swivelling as he looked for a break in the traffic.

Ahead of Colin, the traffic lights turned red and Ron seized his chance. Colin turned the key in the ignition and, once Ron and a few other cars had passed, indicated and started to drive.

'What's the plan, then?' Adam asked.

'We follow Ron to see who he is meeting at 6pm.'

COLIN HAD WATCHED a lot of cop shows on TV. They made it look easy to tail someone without being seen. They always seemed to stay a few cars behind and be able to read the bad guy's mind as to which direction he was going in.

In reality, it was hard work. Colin was nervous that he would lose Ron, thanks to changing traffic lights, straying too far behind and losing sight of him, or getting too close and spooking him.

Thankfully, Colin's car was a run of the mill Hyundai and was unlikely to stand out in amongst the town traffic.

The other thing that the cops seemed to have was a trusting relationship. The driver would be fully in control and his passenger would be 100% behind him.

Colin had Adam, who didn't seem to be 100% behind him. Instead, he nattered in his ear, giving "helpful" hints and tips and droning on about what he'd do. Colin could feel his normally cool demeanour slipping and was thankful that Adam seemed to notice it too, because the backseat driving came to a sudden halt.

They left the town behind and travelled on quieter roads a short distance before Ron indicated into Hamilton's Tavern, a pub just on the outskirts of Stonebridge.

As Ron turned into the car park, Colin stayed on the road, travelling by the pub as if on their way to Meadowfield—the next town over.

When they reached a lay-by, Colin pulled in and they waited a few minutes, before performing a three-point turn and heading back in the direction that they'd come from. When they reached the pub, they turned into the car park and saw Ron's car parked out front, so they chose a space in the bigger car park at the back.

'I can't go in,' Colin said, turning the engine off. 'He saw me earlier and if I just happen to turn up in the same out-of-town pub on the same day, it might around suspicion.'

'You think he'd remember you?' Adam asked.

'No point risking it.'

Secretly, Colin was glad at the prospect of sitting this one out. One encounter with a McNulty was quite enough for one day.

Resigned, Adam got out of the car and disappeared through the back door.

ADAM HAD MADE a fool of himself in Hamilton's more times than he'd care to remember. It was one of those pubs that the under-agers would visit on account of the landlord being a bit loose on the ol' legal age rule. Gordy Hamilton was a legend round these parts.

It had been a while since Adam had visited, though it seemed nothing had changed. The bar ran along one wall, the mirror behind the optics serving to make the place look double the size it actually was. The rest of the space was open plan with misshapen tables taking up much of the floor, though the pool table had been given a reverent place near the front door.

Walking to the bar, Adam clocked Ron McNulty sitting in a little alcove that afforded him an almost unhindered view of the whole room. He was alone, staring at a laptop screen and holding an orange juice. He glanced up at Adam, who gave him a small nod that went unreturned, before lowering his head to his work again.

Adam felt nervous.

He crossed the room, bought a pint, and chose a table as far out of Ron's eyeline as he could. He sat down heavily, playing the part of a tired man who'd just had a hectic day at work. He took a sip of his pint, and then pulled his phone from his pocket.

It was almost six.

With a bit of time on his hands, Adam considered the case so far. As far as he was concerned, Ocean and Willow were involved insomuch as they were part of the same group as Tyler and had both fallen out with him over strategy. As to his demise, Adam was pretty convinced that they had played no part. Sure, they had issues with the dead man, but their lifestyles didn't match up to the violence and hate needed to light a building on fire, knowing someone they knew was inside.

The McNultys weren't likely to set fire to their own property and screw themselves out of a lucrative takeover.

That left Frank Tanner, Mickey and Helena.

Frank had benefitted from the fire financially; Mickey had been assaulted, and worse, by Tyler; and Helena had also been physically abused.

Adam hoped against hope that Helena wasn't involved. He had barely stopped thinking about her since she'd left him alone in the taxi and had resolved to do something about his ongoing singleness (should she be proved innocent).

Thoughts of Helena were pushed from his head by the arrival of Mickey Dooley. He sauntered in through the front door, and stood for a second, surveying the scene in front of him like a cowboy visiting a potentially dangerous tavern for the first time.

Deciding that there was no immediate threat, he strode towards the bar where he chatted to the barmaid for a few minutes before choosing a table once his Guinness had settled. He sat down and pulled his phone out.

At no point did he ever glance over towards the waiting McNulty.

Adam couldn't understand why. Had Ron recognised Adam from somewhere, and called the meeting off? But, if he did that, why would Mickey show up anyway and act as if he didn't know him? Was Mickey waiting for some sort of hand delivered message on a piece of paper? If so, why didn't they just use text message or email? The only reason Adam could think of was that they didn't want to create a digital trail for the police to uncover later.

The scene didn't change for the next thirty minutes.

When it did, it was only because Mickey had finished his pint and decided to call it a night. He walked past Adam without a backwards glance and left via the same door he'd entered.

Adam was going to call it quits soon, too. He felt bad for Colin, having to waste a load of his time sitting in his car.

He tapped on his phone and pulled up his contacts with the intent of calling Colin to quietly relay what he'd seen and ask if they should call it a night. Instead, his eyes fell onto the number from the piece of paper in Tyler's room that he'd saved.

He considered texting but thought better of it. Texting gave someone a chance to block his number or come up with a lie as to who they were.

No. Phoning was the best way forward here. He tapped the number and put the phone to his ear.

'Hello,' a female voice answered after a few rings.

Adam hastily pushed himself out of his seat and walked out of the front door, having realised in the nick of time that declaring who he was and what he was doing within earshot of Ron McNulty would've been a very silly thing to do indeed.

'Hi,' he said, when he was sure he was safely out of range. 'My name is Adam, and I am investigating the death of Tyler Love.'

'I'm Emma,' she said.

'Hi Emma. I was wondering if we could meet to discuss a few things?'

'Are you the police?'

'No. I'm doing a favour for his mum.'

'I don't know anything about how he died.'

'That's fine, but it would still be good to meet. I need as much help as I can get.'

There was a short silence before she agreed.

Tomorrow night. Bar7 at 9pm.

He hung up and re-entered the bar. As he passed the alcove, he saw that Ron was gone.

14

SOLO WORK

THE CRAFT TABLE in the Stonebridge retirement home was a mess. Colin sighed, more for effect than anything. Sometimes it was like clearing up after a bunch of toddlers. He checked his watch and realised that the table had been hastily abandoned because it was time for The Chase—a unanimous favourite amongst the old folk.

As he swept the last of the mess into the bin, Barry approached.

'Alright, Sherlock?' he asked.

'All good,' replied Colin.

'Any news?'

'About the case? Not loads, to be honest. We've prospectively crossed the hippies off our suspect list, but everyone else remains under the spyglass.'

'Have you been up to the warehouse yet?'

'Isn't it still a crime scene?'

'No,' Barry said, shaking his head. 'My daughter drove past it this morning and said all the police tape was down. Might be worth a trip.'

'Don't you think the police will have gone over it with a fine-tooth comb?'

'Not if they only thought the boy killed himself. It was probably only cordoned off for insurance reasons, but I assume all of that has been sorted by now if they've taken their tape down.'

Colin considered this. Perhaps the old man was right—if the police were convinced that Tyler was a lone wolf, they might not have gone to the trouble of searching for another angle. There couldn't be much harm in heading up for a quick look around.

'Cover for me a minute, will you?' he asked.

'Oh, aye,' nodded Barry, tapping the side of his nose conspiratorially.

Colin left the room and ascended the stairs towards the staff room. He pulled his phone from his locker and dialled Adam's number. When he answered, Colin explained his thoughts on what he and Barry had discussed.

'Sounds like a good plan, but I can't do tonight. I'm meeting Emma.'

'No worries. I'll head up myself. I can't imagine there'll be anything to find, but it's worth a shot. Good luck with the girl.'

They hung up with the promise of filling each other in first thing in the morning.

ADAM CHOSE THE same seat by the window and looked up at the bartenders, wondering if they had him pegged as some sort of serial ladies' man. Highly doubtful, he thought, as he looked down at his creased T-shirt.

Like déjà vu, the door to Bar7 opened, though the girl who entered was almost the polar opposite to the one he'd met at the same table a few nights previously. She looked like a surfer, with short, spiky blonde hair, Hurley T-shirt, denim shorts and flip-flops.

She cast an appraising eye over the bar, and Adam stuck his hand in the air to catch her attention. She strolled over and sat down opposite him. Though she was trying her best to appear chilled out, Adam could tell she was nervous. Her eyes were already travelling towards the fire escape door, and her fingertips were drumming a rhythm on the arm of the chair.

'Can I get you a drink?' Adam asked.

She shook her head.

'No, let's just get this over with.' She winced. 'Sorry, that came out unkindly.'

'Not at all,' Adam said. 'It's an odd situation.'

'Actually, maybe I will have a drink,' she said. He watched her vault out of her chair and head to the bar. For a second, he thought she might do a runner, but thankfully she ordered and returned to the table with a half pint of lager.

'What can I do for you?' she asked, after a quick sip.

'Can you tell me how you knew Tyler?'

'We were seeing each other a bit. Nothing serious, no strings.'

'By seeing each other, what do you actually mean?'

She looked at him like he had just spouted two heads.

'What do you think I mean?' she asked.

'I assume... intercourse?'

'And I assume you're not getting any if you are calling it that. Yes, we had *intercourse* a few times. And it was usually when one of us was drunk. In reality, he annoyed the life out of me, but he was good in...'

'I think I've got the picture,' Adam interrupted, not wanting any more detail than he required. 'Did you ever join him at one of the protests?'

She shook her head.

'Why?'

'I've got a job and most of the protests were during the day. Also, I hate antagonising people and that was his whole set up. Even when we were just chilling out together, he'd be trying to turn a chat into a debate. It was exhausting.'

'Sounds it,' Adam nodded, absent-mindedly. His thoughts had drifted to Helena. 'Did you know he had a girlfriend?'

The look on Emma's face told him the answer—a resounding no.

'He never said,' she confirmed. 'Sometimes when we were arranging to see each other, he'd be cagey about his plans for that night, but I just assumed he was up to something with his History Makers group. God, I feel terrible for her. I'm such a bitch.'

Adam shook his head.

'It's not your fault,' he said, consolingly. 'You're not a mind reader. I don't suppose he told you any plans he had for the group?'

'No,' she said. 'He knew I didn't care, so he rarely spoke about it.'

Her tone suggested that she had nothing else to say. She downed her drink and stood up. Adam tried to reassure her that she was not the bad person here, and she nodded, though he could tell she didn't believe him.

He watched her leave and sat down again, considering what this new information meant. It certainly gave Helena more motive if she knew that Tyler had been playing away. Could she really have followed him to the warehouse and set it on fire?

He needed to talk to her again.

He looked at his watch and reckoned that the abrupt end to his meeting with Emma meant that he could meet up with Colin at the warehouse. As he walked to the car, he phoned his friend, and told him he was on his way.

UNDER COVER OF darkness, Colin crept into the skeletal remains of the warehouse. It had been a huge rectangular structure, built from brick in the Victorian times that had now been reduced to mostly rubble. Some of the brickwork did remain, though the walls were now uneven in height and one strong gust of wind away from crumbling completely.

Inside, the devastation caused by the fire was clear to see. The expensive machinery had been reduced to twisted clumps of metal and the floor was littered with warped pieces of wood and tiny fragments of glass that crunched under Colin's feet.

He stood in the vast expanse of destruction and turned a full circle, letting his eyes adjust to the darkness.

Really, as with most of the investigation, he didn't know what he was doing here. He was hoping that something would appear at his feet, or become luminous like in a video game, but he knew that wasn't going to happen, so he got busy.

He skirted the permitter of the building, and worked his way inward. Aside from stopping at various points to take in, up close, the wrath of the flames, he worked quickly.

Nothing jumped out at him.

As he crossed the floor towards what, at one stage, would've been an office, he froze. It might have been his imagination, but he could've sworn that he'd heard something move. He listened intently, though the only sound to break the silence was the roar of a motorbike or a scally in a car with a ridiculous exhaust some way away.

Probably rats, he supposed. The place must be full of them.

When he was happy that he was alone, he moved across the floor and into the office. Just like the main space, in here was destroyed too. What was once a metal filing cabinet was now just a charred husk in the corner of the room and, in the centre, a blackened desk stood on flimsy legs that looked like they could give at any second. Colin was amazed it was upright at all, considering what had happened here.

What had he expected to find? A signed confession from Frank Tanner? Statistical comparisons of how much the McNultys could earn if they claimed on insurance as opposed to agreeing to the multinational deal?

It had been something that Colin had been thinking about since his meeting with Kevin McNulty—how much the man was relying on this insurance pay out, though he knew that he was being unfair. Obviously, insurance existed for a reason, and this was the perfect example.

Kevin had been expecting a huge buyout, and now had to wait on the insurance company to pay out a far smaller sum of money, so that he could house his father in a retirement home and get on with his own life.

The thoughts of Frank, Kevin and insurance were wiped from his mind by another tinkling sound from behind. His mind zoomed back to marauding rodents, but before he could turn to check, all and any thought disappeared, as he was knocked unconscious. The last thing he heard was the sound of fading footsteps before he fell to the floor.

TEN MINUTES LATER, Adam pulled up at the warehouse and got out of his car, using the torch function on his phone to light his path. He climbed over a low wall of bricks and shouted his friend's name but got no answer.

He assumed Colin would've phoned if he'd found something or decided the search was pointless and gone home. Maybe someone had come and escorted Colin off the premises. After all, they were not the police's favourite duo, after solving two crimes the police had decided were accidents. He wondered if DI Whitelaw and his cronies were making sure they weren't bettered a third time.

Adam phoned his friend's number and listened intently. The opening guitar riff of *Back in Black* sounded from somewhere, and he followed Angus Young's tasty licks like a beacon through the darkness.

The music cut off when Colin's phone went to voicemail, but by then Adam's eyes had fallen on his friend.

Colin was lying in a side room surrounded by splintered wood, face down as if he had been dropped though the table from a great height.

Adam ran to his friend's side, and despite the blood (he was notoriously bad at dealing with claret), checked Colin's pulse. Thankfully, there was one. There was also a huge gash on the back of his head that required urgent attention.

Summoning all his courage, Adam hoisted Colin to his feet and put his arm around him. It looked like they were taking part in some sort of Battle Royale style three-legged race.

Halfway across the floor, Colin came to, though very groggily.

'Wha 'appen?' he asked, his speech slurred.

'We're getting you to the hospital,' Adam replied, before whispering to himself, 'and then I'm going to kill the son of a bitch who did this to you.'

15

THE OLD FAMILIAR STING

ADAM HAD ALWAYS hated hospitals.

The drab paintwork and the overhead strip lighting caused everyone to look ill, even if they weren't. His fear was always that a doctor would mistake him for a sick person and wrongfully administer some sort of drug. He knew that it was stupidly irrational and had never voiced it aloud.

The door of the waiting room flapped open and in walked another worried plus-one, who fell into a chair opposite him, offering no greeting, which suited Adam just fine. All his thoughts were taken up by the wellbeing of his friend.

Thankfully, Colin's mental capacities had improved in the car. He couldn't remember anything about who had attacked him, except that they must've been there since he'd arrived, since they had squirrelled themselves away in that side office where Adam had found him.

Colin had then faded into silence, focussed on holding one of the McDonald's napkins Adam had found in the passenger footwell to the cut on his head.

Adam had used the quiet to reflect on what had happened. Had whoever been hiding in the building been on a cover-up mission? Perhaps Frank Tanner had snuck in, just to make sure he'd left nothing incriminating behind that the police had missed.

Frustrated, Adam stood and left the room. He headed down the corridor towards the café, though it was shut when he got there. Instead, he turned to the bank of vending machines and chose a bar of chocolate and a bag of cheese and onion Tayto crisps. Until he tore the wrapper of his Twix, he hadn't realised how hungry he was.

He sat down on a nearby seat and munched his way through the snacks. His thoughts turned back to the McNultys. Colin had mentioned something about insurance, but Adam didn't buy that angle. It was too obvious. They were psychos, but they weren't stupid.

Which left Helena.

Could she have been the one wielding the length of wood that had caused Colin to black out?

Adam sighed and stood to put his rubbish in the bin. He looked back up the corridor and froze.

There she was.

Helena.

He spun around, planting his back against the wall like Solid Snake used to do in Metal Gear Solid. He peered out again, getting a better look at his target.

Helena's hair was tied up in a neat bun and she wore matching navy top and trousers. She was linked arm-in-arm with an old man wearing a gown and holding onto one of those portable poles with a fluid bag attached to the top.

Adam did the maths. Either she was pretending to be a nurse, sneaking in covertly to the hospital to finish putting Colin's lights out and was taking her undercover role very seriously, or she really was a nurse.

The last option sounded more plausible. She had probably mentioned it when they were drinking at Bar7, but the effects of the alcohol had more than likely been playing with his memory by that point.

Adam left his position and started to walk up the corridor towards her, pretending he hadn't noticed her. As he passed, he glanced up and saw the recognition in her eyes.

'Adam?' she said.

'Ah, Helena! How are you?' he asked, acting surprised.

'Is this your boyfriend?' the old man asked.

'I was about to ask her the same question,' Adam joked, eliciting a bark of laughter from the old man.

'No, just a friend,' she told him, before turning to Adam. 'Let me get Larry back to his room and then we'll catch up.'

Adam watched her slow journey towards the patient's ward. She pushed the door open and let the old man enter first. A few moments later, she reappeared, alone and beckoned Adam towards a side room.

'What are you doing here?' she asked. 'Is everything okay?'

'My friend got beaten up.'

'That's awful,' she said, raising her hands to her cheeks. 'Is this something to do with Tyler?'

'What time did you start working today?' he asked, instead of answering her question. Adam didn't know if he could trust her.

'I started at seven o'clock. I'm here for the night shift. And I know what you are thinking, and like I told you already, I didn't have anything to do with Tyler's death, nor did I have anything to do with your friend getting beaten up.'

'Sorry.'

'It's okay. I know you're trying to do a good thing, but I'm hurting too. Tyler and I were coming to the end of the line, but it doesn't mean I wanted anything bad to happen to him.'

Adam considered what he'd learned earlier, about Tyler and Emma getting together while he was still in a relationship with Helena. A few hours ago, Emma's news had put Helena firmly in the frame, but now that he knew she had nothing to do with hurting Colin, he also was convinced she wasn't involved in Tyler's death.

'What is it?' she asked, breaking the silence.

'I've got something to ask you that might be upsetting…' he replied.

'Go on.'

'Did you know that Tyler was cheating on you?'

'No,' she said, shaking her head sadly. 'Though, it would explain an awful lot. How did you find out?'

'I found a phone number in his room and met up with the owner tonight to ask some questions.'

'And you thought that if I knew he'd been cheating, that might be another reason why I'd want to kill him?'

Adam looked uneasy.

'Jesus,' she said. 'I need a drink.'

'Tomorrow night?' he asked, though he knew his timing wasn't the best. Asking someone out on a date soon after accusing them of murder and informing them that they'd been cheated on wasn't exactly ideal.

'I'm sorry,' she said, shaking her head. 'It's not a good time.'

With that, she opened the door and left him alone with his shame.

WHEN HE WAS sure that his cheeks weren't illuminated like beacons anymore, he walked out into the corridor and headed in the direction of the waiting room. To his surprise, Colin was sat in one of the chairs. His head was wrapped in a bandage, though he looked much more with it.

They left the hospital together and headed for Adam's car. The night air was crisp and served as a welcome respite to the stuffy, germ-filled air of the hospital.

Once they were seated, Adam spoke.

'I think we should give up. To my mind, the hippies aren't involved, and neither is Helena. Which leaves the McNultys, Frank Tanner or Mickey Dooley. They're all scary boys, and ones I don't think we should be messing with.'

'Nah,' Colin said, shaking his head. 'I want to find whichever bastard did this to me and teach them a lesson.'

'That's the concussion talking,' Adam said. 'Do you think your mum is going to let you keep going?'

'We're 25 Adam. I don't have to listen to my mum!'

16

NO REST FOR THE WICKED

COLIN HAD HAD a dreadful night's sleep. Each time, just as he'd get comfortable, pain flared through his head like a jolt of electricity. He'd cursed the weak painkillers he'd been given and had resigned himself to a night of being awake. Thankfully, at some stage, his need for rest had overruled the pain and now, he woke slowly with drool running down the side of his cheek.

He sat up slowly and took in his battered reflection in the mirror. The bandage wrapped around his head wasn't a great look, and the constellation of cuts on his face looked even worse. If there was a silver lining, it was that he hadn't lost any teeth.

Or died. *That* was probably the golden lining.

He got out of bed and went downstairs to get breakfast. It was on days like today that he was happy he no longer lived with his parents. If he did, the amount of explaining he'd have to do would be ridiculous. If he could only avoid them for a week or so, they might never have to find out about his beating.

He was also thankful that it was his day off. He planned on spending the day in bed, watching telly and resting. In fact, he was going to treat himself to jammy toast in bed. The only shame was that he'd have to make it himself. Or, he could call Adam…

No.

Having your friend bring you food in bed was too weird.

Once the toast was coated in strawberry jam, he took his plate and glass of orange juice up the stairs with him, propped the pillows up against the headboard and got in, pulling the duvet up to his neck.

He thought about what Adam said, about leaving the case be. It was definitely the smart move—the stitches in the back of his head were testament to that.

But, the ending felt close. The pool of suspects was being whittled down and Colin couldn't help but feel that the answer was close at hand. The throbbing in his head was arguing that they had perhaps got *too* close.

He breathed out deeply and resolved to spend today resting. The case would not enter his mind from now on.

As he thought this, his phone rang. He looked at the display and was dismayed to find that it was the retirement home.

'Hello,' he answered.

'Colin, it's Mary. I know it's your day off, but we've just had a viewing appointment booked and the man asked for you specifically.'

'Who is it?' Colin asked, though he already knew.

'Kevin McNulty.'

Colin assured Mary that he'd be in for the appointment at three before hanging up.

So much for a day of rest and not thinking about the case.

COLIN ARRIVED EARLY so that his colleagues and the old folk could get their shock at his appearance out of their systems.

He assured them that it had been caused by a freak accident, and that it wasn't as bad as it looked. In reality, now that he was up and about, it felt like a hangover from hell. It was only when he had a quiet moment alone with Barry that he admitted how rough he felt.

'You're getting somewhere, then,' the old man said.

'What do you mean?'

'Well, lashing out is the mark of a man who feels cornered. And someone certainly lashed out at you. And now we've got a visit from a McNulty. Do you think the two events are connected?'

'Doubtful,' Colin said. 'If he battered me, why would he ask for me to show him around?'

'Good point. That's why you're the detective and not me.'

Mary poked her head around the frame of the door and told Colin that the visitors were here.

'You need back up, you let me know,' Barry said, adopting a boxing stance, just as he descended into a huge coughing fit.

'Aye, I'll keep that in mind, Ali,' Colin said, as he left the room.

He met Kevin McNulty and his father, Raymond, at reception, greeting them with a handshake. Kevin glanced up at Colin's bandage, and Colin felt a silly impulse to apologise for how unsightly he looked.

'Did one of this lot do that to you?' Kevin asked with a smile, motioning to the roomful of OAPs.

'Yeah,' Colin said, 'Geraldine hates it when I'm late with her lunch. Isn't that right, Ger?'

'Too right,' she replied. 'Especially on lasagne day.'

Colin led Kevin and Raymond through the day room, chatting to them about the facilities, the range of activities on offer and introducing them to some of the folk who weren't asleep in one of the cosy armchairs dotted around the room.

He led them to the vacant bedroom that would be Raymond's if he wanted it. Raymond walked in, and the other two gave him some space and time. This part of the job often hit Colin like an emotional car crash. It was the point at which the elderly gent or lady knew that their independence was coming to an end. Some accepted it with a stoic nod, some saw it as a new adventure and looked genuinely excited at the prospect while others looked like a devastated child being abandoned on the first day of school.

Ray was the former. He glanced around dispassionately, pushing into the mattress with a balled fist to check its springiness before taking in the view from the window.

'Has the insurance money come through?' Colin asked Kevin.

'Not yet,' he said. 'But it should be any day now, and we thought it best to be prepared. I assume there will be some sort of administration involved on your end that could take a while so we thought we'd come and have a look around and start making decisions.'

Kevin's phone started ringing in his pocket, and he checked the display before excusing himself. Colin watched him walk down the corridor with purpose, before pushing through the doors at the end that led to reception.

'What do you think, then?' Colin asked, turning his attention to Raymond.

'It'll do,' he replied, sitting down on the desk chair.

'It's daunting at the start, but you'll soon make friends.'

He nodded, and Colin worried that he'd sounded patronising.

'I imagine your sons will come and visit often, too.'

The old man laughed. 'You must be joking. If you asked Ron who his father was, he'd tell you he didn't have one.'

'Why?' Colin blurted out, before he could help himself. 'Sorry, that's a bit personal.'

'You're fine, son. It's because you should never mix family and business. You see, when I was coming up to retirement age, I gave the business to the boys. It was my father's before me and his father's before that, and then it passed to me and my brother. Because I was older, I got 75% share.'

'Didn't that cause arguments?'

'Some, but it was a family tradition. Happened in every generation. My father once explained that it was so there was an outright leader. Someone who the buck stopped with. And, so, I continued it. Ron thought I might be the one to break the tradition, to split it 50/50.'

'But you didn't?'

'I didn't. Tradition is tradition.'

'So it's mostly Kevin who you see?'

'It's only Kevin I see,' Raymond said. 'Ron has effectively disowned me. Though, I suspect if their deal had gone through, and he'd made his fortune, he'd have got in touch to rub it in my face.'

'Were you upset that they were selling the business?'

He leaned back a little in the chair, his expression suggesting it was the first time he'd thought about it.

'I suppose I was. It's been in the family for generations now. One of the oldest butchers on the north coast, alongside Tanner's. It would've been a shame to see the abattoir with someone else's name on it.'

Colin's attention was stolen by the re-appearance of Kevin striding up the corridor. He smiled warmly and, when he reached them, poked his head around the door.

'Looks like you've got yourself settled already,' he said to his dad, who didn't bother to hide his eyeroll.

When Raymond had seen enough, Colin led them back to the reception area. Kevin told him that they'd be in touch soon and shook his hand. Raymond gave him a small smile and they departed.

Colin watched them go, keenly aware that Kevin could've been the one who'd bashed him over the head last night. He also couldn't wait to tell Adam what he'd managed to find out from Raymond.

He watched the McNultys climb into their car and leave the car park. When he was sure they were gone, Colin left too.

ADAM PUT DOWN the phone and thought about what Colin had just told him.

Colin's theory about insurance had been spinning through his mind all day. He'd sped through his work that morning, probably doing a horrific job on Mrs Kedie's flowerbeds, though she was partially blind, and he could nip back and fix them before she realised. Once he'd packed his gear into the van, he'd driven home and spent the day doing a bit of research.

He felt like Colin's information lent further credence to his idea, but it was like doing a jigsaw and finding that some crucial parts hadn't been cut quite right. Nothing was fitting together properly.

Yet.

But he had a plan.

If this were a film, there'd be a montage showing a flurry of action. In reality, Adam needed to print a few things and the sodding printer jammed. He spent a few minutes cursing it to high heaven in the hope that insults alone would jolt it into action, and when that didn't work, he turned it off and on again which only made the damned thing chew up his last few pieces of paper.

His gave it the middle finger, and in reply a notification flashed up informing him that it was out of ink.

He unplugged the leads from his laptop and gathered up anything else he'd need, before pulling out his phone and ringing Colin back.

'Are you at home?' he asked.

'I will be in five minutes.'

'Is your printer set up?'

'Yeah, why?'

'I need to print something, obviously, and mine is doing the devil's work. See you in fifteen.'

With that, he hung up, grabbed his keys from the sideboard and marched towards the door.

It was business time.

17

WHOLE LOTTA LUCK

'I THOUGHT YOU said yours was working?' Adam said. A purple vein was throbbing in his forehead.

'It was the last time I used it. It's you and your bad printer juju that making it go on the fritz.'

'Well, we need to print this off somehow so that we can present the information, but I can just show you for now.'

Adam turned the laptop screen towards his friend and talked through what he'd found. Colin listened intently, despite the throbbing pain in the back of his head. The information was coming thick and fast, though when Adam had finished, he was convinced that they'd arrived at the correct outcome.

'So what do we do now?' Colin asked.

'We somehow lure them to a meeting place. Somewhere public so that they can't hurt us.'

Colin left the room and walked to the kitchen. Hr grabbed a packet of paracetamol from the drawer and poured a glass of water, throwing the tablets back in quick order. He was impressed with Adam's investigating, but didn't want to let on too much. He could already feel his friend's ego swelling.

Keen to contribute, he racked his brain for a kernel of an idea. Something that could bridge the next step…

'I've got it,' he shouted, shocking himself.

'What?'

'I have an idea as to how we can get them to a meeting point.'

Colin explained his idea, and was annoyed when Adam pointed out the gaping holes. After a few minutes of knocking ideas back and forward, they'd figured how to paper over some of the cracks, though they'd still need a hell of a lot of luck.

Adam pulled his laptop towards him and started on his side of the plan while Colin grabbed his keys and headed to town.

AN HOUR LATER, they had what they needed.

Adam was in possession of two mobile phone numbers, which he had scribbled on a piece of paper. He slid it across the table to Colin, who picked it up and keyed the first number into the brand-new phone he was holding.

"Brand-new" in the fact that he had bought it within the last sixty minutes. It had cost fifteen quid from the exchange shop and would have been considered behind-the-times in 2002. Still, he only needed to send two messages and it was more than capable of that.

'Before I send this, are we sure that there isn't a more fool-proof way of getting them both there?'

'Nope,' Adam said, shaking his head. 'I tried to come up with something better when you were out, but nothing came.'

'Great.'

Typing on something other than an iPhone felt strange. The phone didn't have a touch screen so he had to use the number buttons to painstakingly spell out the words. It was like typing morse code.

He finished typing and passed the phone to Adam to check it before he pressed send. Adam read it aloud.

'I think someone is on to us. Usual place. 6pm. No contact until then.'

Adam looked up from the phone and nodded, though Colin could see that he still wasn't fully convinced. Before they could chicken out, Colin grabbed the phone off him and hit the send button. He then typed an identical message and sent it to the second number.

When he was sure the duplicate message had been delivered, he took the back off the phone and popped the battery and SIM card out. He shoved the former in the bin and snapped the latter in half.

He then set the phone onto the carpet and stood on it with a heavy boot.

'Who do you think you are? The SAS?' Adam laughed.

'Dunno. It feels like something Jack Bauer would do,' Colin shrugged. 'Now, we need a great big slice of luck.'

And, as if a message was being sent from the heavens, Colin's printer beeped to life and began delivering the pages Adam had sent an hour ago.

'Fate smiles upon us,' Adam said.

Colin rolled his eyes.

18

USUAL PLACE. 6PM. ENCORE.

COLIN AND ADAM pulled into Hamilton's at five o'clock, keen to get there early and secure a good seat.

The plan was set. The hope was that the two guilty men would think the other had texted them, and that they'd both show up to find out what intelligence the other had gathered. Then, Colin and Adam would swoop in.

So as not to arouse suspicion, they went to the bar and ordered a beer each, and some food. Colin opted for the fabled surf and turf, while Adam went for the burger. They carried their drinks to the corner table and waited.

A short while later, the food arrived and, just before six, the first of the men entered.

Ron McNulty went straight to the alcove and sat down, casting a sneaky glance around the room before pulling his laptop out. Adam assumed he was pretending to do work; something to make it look like he was here for a reason.

The barman brought a pint of lager to him, which he accepted with a fake smile, though it sat untouched on the table while Ron's eyes flicked towards the door every couple of seconds.

Ten minutes later, Colin and Adam's suspicions were confirmed to be true. The next man through the door was Frank Tanner. He glanced around furtively, before heading straight to the table occupied by Ron, sliding into the chair beside him.

Adam could hear irritated mutterings, though couldn't make out what they were saying.

'Time?' he said to Colin.

'None like the present.'

They got out of their seats and crossed the room. It was empty, aside from the four men, the barman, and a curly haired fella reading the newspaper with his back to them, oblivious to the fireworks that were about to be lit.

'Evening gents,' said Adam, summoning more nerve than he thought he had in him. 'Mind if we sit?'

Without waiting for an answer, he slid into the chair opposite Ron. Colin followed his lead, taking the last remaining seat.

'Gentlemen, we have much to discuss. You see, we know what you've got yourself muddled up in.'

'And what would that be?' asked Ron.

'Oh, let's see… we've uncovered insurance fraud and manslaughter so far, but who knows where that list ends.'

'Is this about the fire?' Ron asked. 'The fire that destroyed my business? I'm the victim here, Mr…?'

'Never you worry about our names for now. And labelling yourself the victim here is laughable. *He*,' Adam pointed at Frank, 'could be considered the victim, at a stretch, but only because he's got as many braincells as one of those chickens he makes his living from. But, you? I think *mastermind* might be the best label for you.'

Frank looked confused by what was going on. He stared dumbly at Ron, who seemed to be the mouthpiece of this alliance.

'And who do you think the police are going to believe? They were the ones that told me the fire was caused by that wee lad who died.'

'Tyler Love. We'll get to him,' Adam replied. 'He's the reason we got involved in the first place.'

'What are you? Private detectives?' Ron laughed. 'Dicks, they sometimes get called, don't they? Well, if the shoe fits...'

Adam ignored the childish jibe and set the manila folder on the table. Ron adopted a bored look, though Adam could tell his interest had been piqued.

'Here's what we'll do. I'll present my case, you tell me if I'm hot or cold, and at the end we'll see if I've won the speedboat.'

Ron looked bemused, not least by the Bullseye reference.

'Here goes. Tyler's mum asked us to look into his death. She didn't believe the police—told us he wasn't the type of boy to go around lighting fires. Now, I'll be honest, we talked to a fair few people about him and not many had positive words to say. Still, going from petty vandalism to arson is a leap, so we looked at other avenues.

'The stroke of luck came when we spoke to your father. He told us about the crappy deal you we're getting. twenty five percent of the family business because you were born a few years later than your brother is a bit of a bum deal. My words, not his. He fully stood by his decision, isn't that right, Colin?'

'Bang on,' Colin agreed.

'So, even with the multinational buying your business, you weren't going to make as much from it. Why take a quarter of that pie, when you could have half of another.'

Adam reached into the manila folder and pulled out a piece of paper.

'After your bit of street theatre the other day, when Frank came to speak to you at your office, we thought something was amiss. I mean, why would Frank be coming to speak to you? You hate each other, right?'

'Wrong, it would seem,' Colin continued. 'But you didn't want your brother to know that, so you took Frank out onto the street and gave him a bit of a fake duffing…'

'It wasn't fake,' Frank interjected. 'He smacked me in the bloody stomach.'

'Regardless,' Colin said. 'We figured you two were working together, so we looked into a few things. It seems that you, Ron, bought some shares in Frank's business not so long ago. Quite a lot, actually. Half of the company. And, you probably got quite a good deal when you told Frank of your plan.'

Ron didn't say anything, but Adam noted a look of fear cross his face for the first time. He was on the ropes.

'Now, all you needed to do was make sure the McNulty Meats deal didn't go through. So you burned your business to the ground.'

'Ah, that's where you're wrong,' he started, though Adam shut him down.

'Figure of speech. I should've said the business was burned to the ground. By Frank. You knew that if anyone saw you do it, the insurance wouldn't pay out. So, you instructed Frank to do it, and like an obedient little boy, he did.'

Neither Ron nor Frank said a word.

'So, now with McNulty Meats in ashes, the multinational moved onto the next biggest company in Stonebridge. What luck. Now, Ron and Frank are going to be rich, and Ron even has that 25% of the insurance pay out winging its way to him, too!'

'Tragically,' Colin said, taking up the story. 'Unbeknown to you, Tyler had broken into your factory and was tinkering with your machinery, or smashing windows or something. Revenge for you roughing him up at the protest. Frank chucks the petrol bomb in, Tyler can't escape, and a young man dies.'

'A thug,' Ron spits.

'A dead one. It must've been such a relief when the police blamed him. I bet you thought you were home and dry, eh? So, how did we do?'

'Clean sweep, if I'm honest, lads. What can I say? I was getting the crap end of the shovel with my father's outdated business decisions. I worked my fingers to the bone for the company, in the hope that he'd change his mind. When he didn't, I took matters into my own hands. Tyler's death was a mistake, but he shouldn't have broken into the warehouse.'

Ron lifted his pint for the first time and took a hearty slug, before slamming it roughly back onto the table. He wiped his top lip and smiled.

'Now, as interesting as that was, hearing you two boy scouts recounting my plan back to me, it was all for nothing. The police think Tyler did it, and just because I invested in another business does not show me as guilty. In fact, it showcases my entrepreneurial spirit and community-mindedness, if anything. Why are the police going to believe you two?'

AT THAT MOMENT, the curly haired man sitting at the bar folded his newspaper and spun round on the seat.

'I'd say hearing a full confession with my own ears might be reason enough,' Detective Inspector Whitelaw said. He spoke into the walkie-talkie that was attached to his shirt pocket, and suddenly the bar was swarming with police officers.

'One more question,' Colin said, while the two men were being handcuffed. 'Which one of you bashed me over the head?'

Ron and Frank both genuinely looked blank.

'Take them away,' Whitelaw ordered, before turning to Adam and Colin and offering congratulations, albeit begrudgingly.

WHEN THE MADNESS had died down, Colin and Adam retook their places at the corner table they'd chosen originally. They ordered fresh pints, and when they came, clinked them together.

'Surely,' Colin said, 'that's Stonebridge's quota of drama filled for the foreseeable future.'

'You'd think,' Adam agreed.

19

AN ANSWER AND A QUESTION

THEY WERE BOTH wrong. Stonebridge wasn't quite finished with them yet.

Colin walked down the street, glad that he and Adam had called it quits after pint four. His mum had Facetimed earlier that morning, and, forgetting that he looked like a battered potato, had pressed the green button.

Her gasp had shocked him. She'd been at once angry, confused, cross and weepy. She'd made him tell her everything, and admonished him for keeping it a secret. He'd felt bad, and had proposed meeting for lunch to tell her the whole story.

As he passed the town hall, he saw Mickey, and nodded. He was speaking into his microphone, trying to entice passers-by to listen, but no one seemed interested today. When Mickey saw Colin, he froze. For a second, Colin thought he was having one of those absence seizures, but then he dropped the microphone, causing the town square to fill with squealing feedback.

Mickey turned his PA system off and ran over to Colin.

'Dude,' he said. 'I owe you an apology.'

Mickey told Colin how he had been up at the McNulty warehouse the other night, looking for any evidence that they'd been up to no good. After his and Colin's chat, he'd felt bad about dissing Tyler, so had set about trying to help Colin and Adam's investigation in order to exonerate his old foe.

Mickey had been in the office when he'd heard someone come in to the warehouse. He suspected it was one of the McNultys, so had armed himself with a table leg. He'd bashed Colin over the head with it, and ran.

He rained apologies down on Colin who waved them away. Colin assured Mickey that he would've done the same before giving Mickey a brief overview of what he and Adam had uncovered. After that, they bade each other goodbye.

Colin walked away, happy in the knowledge that the final mystery had been solved. He also determined never to get on Mickey's bad side!

ACROSS TOWN, Adam was regretting that fourth pint. His head was a mess.

He pulled himself out of bed and walked down the stairs, hunting for some paracetamol. He popped two out of the blister packet and set them on the counter, before reaching into the cupboard and pulling out a mug. He set it on the counter, too. As he pulled his hand away, something caught his eye.

There was movement inside the mug, so instinctively, he punched it, smashing it completely.

As the pain registered in his shrapnel-bitten hand, two things went through his mind. Firstly, that punching the mug because he thought a spider was inside it was a silly thing to do, and secondly, he was most likely going to need stitches.

Luckily, he'd fallen asleep in last night's clothes.

He grabbed a jacket off the coat hook and, summoning every ounce of bravery in his body, wrapped it around his bleeding hand, putting as much pressure on it as he could stand. He made his way to the car and drove carefully to the hospital.

When he got there, he paid through the nose for a car parking ticket, sticking it begrudgingly onto his windscreen before making his way into A&E. He told the receptionist why he was here, and she told him to take a seat; that someone would be with him shortly.

He strolled to the seat, hungover, trying not to think about how much blood he was losing. Things couldn't get any worse, he thought, glumly.

'Adam?'

Ah! Things *could* get worse, it would seem.

Helena stood in the doorway of one of the treatment rooms. Even in her work garb, she looked beautiful. Adam cursed the universe.

She beckoned him towards her and led him into the room. He unfurled the jacket and showed her his injury, explaining what had happened. His face was burning with embarrassment. 'Adam, this is a bit extreme,' she winked. 'If you wanted to ask me out again, you could've just phoned.'

ABOUT THE AUTHOR

Originally hailing from the north coast of Northern Ireland and now residing in South Manchester, Chris McDonald has always been a reader. At primary school, The Hardy Boys inspired his love of adventure, before his reading world was opened up by Chuck Palahniuk and the gritty world of crime.

He's a fan of 5-a-side football, has an eclectic taste in music ranging from Damien Rice to Slayer and loves dogs.